Mary. A Fiction by Mary Wollstonecraft

Mary Wollstonecraft was born on 27th April 1759 in Spitalfields, London. Although her family had a comfortable income much was squandered by her father leading the family to become financially diminished. Wollstonecraft struck out on her own in 1778 and accepted a job as a lady's companion. Frustrated by the limited career options open to respectable yet poor women, she nonetheless decided to embark upon a career as an author. At the time, few women could support themselves by writing.

She learned French and German and translated texts. She also wrote reviews, primarily of novels, for Johnson's periodical, the Analytical Review.

Wollstonecraft also pursued a relationship with the artist Henry Fuseli. Boldly she proposed a platonic living arrangement with Fuseli and his wife. Fuseli's wife was shocked and the relationship was severed.

In December 1792 she left for France to view first hand the revolutionary events that she had just celebrated in her recent 'Vindication of the Rights of Men' (1790) and that had brought her immediate fame.

France declared war on Britain in February 1793 and Wollstonecraft tried to leave for Switzerland but was denied permission. Despite her sympathy for the revolution, life for Wollstonecraft was very uncomfortable.

Having just written the 'Rights of Woman', Wollstonecraft determined to put her ideas to the test. She alighted on and fell passionately in love with Gilbert Imlay, an American diplomat and adventurer. By now she was disillusioned by the Revolution's path. She thought the republic behaved slavishly to those in power while the government was 'venal' and 'brutal'. To protect Wollstonecraft from the prospect of arrest, Imlay made a false statement to the U.S. embassy in Paris that he had married her, automatically making her an American citizen. Wollstonecraft, now pregnant by Imlay, gave birth to her first child, Fanny, on 14th May 1794. She was overjoyed.

The winter of 1794–95 was the coldest winter in over a century. Wollstonecraft and Fanny were reduced to desperate circumstances. Wollstonecraft now had to risk leaving France and did so on 7th April 1795. She sought Imlay out but he was impassive to her pleas. In May 1795 she attempted to commit suicide, but it is thought Imlay saved her life. But it was now certain that her relationship with Imlay was over. She attempted suicide for a second time but a passing stranger witnessed her jump into the Thames and rescued her.

Gradually, Wollstonecraft returned to literary life, and to a relationship with William Godwin. Once Wollstonecraft became pregnant by him, they decided to marry so that the child would be legitimate.

On 30th August 1797, Wollstonecraft gave birth to her second daughter, Mary. During the delivery the placenta broke apart and became infected. After several days of agony, Mary Wollstonecraft died of septicemia on 10th September 1797.

Index of Contents

ADVERTISEMENT

In delineating the Heroine of this Fiction, the Author attempts to develop a character different from those generally portrayed. This woman is neither a Clarissa, a Lady G—, nor a* Sophie.—It would be vain to mention the various modifications of these models, as it would to remark, how widely artists wander from nature, when they copy the originals of great masters. They catch the gross parts; but the subtle spirit evaporates; and not having the just ties, affectation disgusts, when grace was expected to charm.

Those compositions only have power to delight, and carry us willing captives, where the soul of the author is exhibited, and animates the hidden springs. Lost in a pleasing enthusiasm, they live in the scenes they represent; and do not measure their steps in a beaten track, solicitous to gather expected flowers, and bind them in a wreath, according to the prescribed rules of art.

These chosen few, wish to speak for themselves, and not to be an echo—even of the sweetest sounds— or the reflector of the most sublime beams. The** paradise they ramble in, must be of their own creating—or the prospect soon grows insipid, and not varied by a vivifying principle, fades and dies.

In an artless tale, without episodes, the mind of a woman, who has thinking powers is displayed. The female organs have been thought too weak for this arduous employment; and experience seems to justify the assertion. Without arguing physically about possibilities—in a fiction, such a being may be allowed to exist; whose grandeur is derived from the operations of its own faculties, not subjugated to opinion; but drawn by the individual from the original source.

FOOTNOTES:
*Rousseau.
**I here give the Reviewers an opportunity of being very witty about the Paradise of Fools, &c.

MARY

CHAPTER I

Mary, the heroine of this fiction, was the daughter of Edward, who married Eliza, a gentle, fashionable girl, with a kind of indolence in her temper, which might be termed negative good-nature: her virtues, indeed, were all of that stamp. She carefully attended to the shews of things, and her opinions, I should have said prejudices, were such as the generality approved of. She was educated with the expectation of a large fortune, of course became a mere machine: the homage of her attendants made a great part of her puerile amusements, and she never imagined there were any relative duties for her to fulfil: notions of her own consequence, by these means, were interwoven in her mind, and the years of youth spent in acquiring a few superficial accomplishments, without having any taste for them. When she was first introduced into the polite circle, she danced with an officer, whom she faintly wished to be united to; but her father soon after recommending another in a more distinguished rank of life, she readily submitted to his will, and promised to love, honour, and obey, (a vicious fool,) as in duty bound.

While they resided in London, they lived in the usual fashionable style, and seldom saw each other; nor were they much more sociable when they wooed rural felicity for more than half the year, in a delightful country, where Nature, with lavish hand, had scattered beauties around; for the master, with brute, unconscious gaze, passed them by unobserved, and sought amusement in country sports. He hunted in the morning, and after eating an immoderate dinner, generally fell asleep: this seasonable rest enabled him to digest the cumbrous load; he would then visit some of his pretty tenants; and when he compared their ruddy glow of health with his wife's countenance, which even rouge could not enliven, it is not necessary to say which a gourmand would give the preference to. Their vulgar dance of spirits were infinitely more agreeable to his fancy than her sickly, die-away languor. Her voice was but the shadow of a sound, and she had, to complete her delicacy, so relaxed her nerves, that she became a mere nothing.

Many such noughts are there in the female world! yet she had a good opinion of her own merit,—truly, she said long prayers,—and sometimes read her Week's Preparation: she dreaded that horrid place vulgarly called hell, the regions below; but whether her's was a mounting spirit, I cannot pretend to determine; or what sort of a planet would have been proper for her, when she left her material part in this world, let metaphysicians settle; I have nothing to say to her unclothed spirit.

As she was sometimes obliged to be alone, or only with her French waiting-maid, she sent to the metropolis for all the new publications, and while she was dressing her hair, and she could turn her eyes from the glass, she ran over those most delightful substitutes for bodily dissipation, novels. I say bodily, or the animal soul, for a rational one can find no employment in polite circles. The glare of lights, the studied inelegancies of dress, and the compliments offered up at the shrine of false beauty, are all equally addressed to the senses.

When she could not any longer indulge the caprices of fancy one way, she tried another. The Platonic Marriage, Eliza Warwick, and some other interesting tales were perused with eagerness. Nothing could be more natural than the developement of the passions, nor more striking than the views of the human heart. What delicate struggles! and uncommonly pretty turns of thought! The picture that was found on a bramble-bush, the new sensitive-plant, or tree, which caught the swain by the upper-garment, and presented to his ravished eyes a portrait.—Fatal image!—It planted a thorn in a till then insensible heart, and sent a new kind of a knight-errant into the world. But even this was nothing to the catastrophe, and the circumstance on which it hung, the hornet settling on the sleeping lover's face. What a heart-rending accident! She planted, in imitation of those susceptible souls, a rose bush; but there was not a lover to weep in concert with her, when she watered it with her tears.—Alas! Alas!

If my readers would excuse the sportiveness of fancy, and give me credit for genius, I would go on and tell them such tales as would force the sweet tears of sensibility to flow in copious showers down beautiful cheeks, to the discomposure of rouge, &c. &c. Nay, I would make it so interesting, that the fair peruser should beg the hair-dresser to settle the curls himself, and not interrupt her.

She had besides another resource, two most beautiful dogs, who shared her bed, and reclined on cushions near her all the day. These she watched with the most assiduous care, and bestowed on them the warmest caresses. This fondness for animals was not that kind of attendrissement which makes a person take pleasure in providing for the subsistence and comfort of a living creature; but it proceeded from vanity, it gave her an opportunity of lisping out the prettiest French expressions of ecstatic fondness, in accents that had never been attuned by tenderness.

She was chaste, according to the vulgar acceptation of the word, that is, she did not make any actual faux pas; she feared the world, and was indolent; but then, to make amends for this seeming self-denial, she read all the sentimental novels, dwelt on the love-scenes, and, had she thought while she read, her mind would have been contaminated; as she accompanied the lovers to the lonely arbors, and would walk with them by the clear light of the moon. She wondered her husband did not stay at home. She was jealous—why did he not love her, sit by her side, squeeze her hand, and look unutterable things? Gentle reader, I will tell thee; they neither of them felt what they could not utter. I will not pretend to say that they always annexed an idea to a word; but they had none of those feelings which are not easily analyzed.

CHAPTER II

In due time she brought forth a son, a feeble babe; and the following year a daughter. After the mother's throes she felt very few sentiments of maternal tenderness: the children were given to nurses, and she played with her dogs. Want of exercise prevented the least chance of her recovering strength; and two or three milk-fevers brought on a consumption, to which her constitution tended. Her children all died in their infancy, except the two first, and she began to grow fond of the son, as he was remarkably handsome. For years she divided her time between the sofa, and the card-table. She thought not of death, though on the borders of the grave; nor did any of the duties of her station occur to her as necessary. Her children were left in the nursery; and when Mary, the little blushing girl, appeared, she would send the awkward thing away. To own the truth, she was awkward enough, in a house without any play-mates; for her brother had been sent to school, and she scarcely knew how to employ herself; she would ramble about the garden, admire the flowers, and play with the dogs. An old house-keeper told her stories, read to her, and, at last, taught her to read. Her mother talked of enquiring for a governess when her health would permit; and, in the interim desired her own maid to teach her French. As she had learned to read, she perused with avidity every book that came in her way. Neglected in every respect, and left to the operations of her own mind, she considered every thing that came under her inspection, and learned to think. She had heard of a separate state, and that angels sometimes visited this earth. She would sit in a thick wood in the park, and talk to them; make little songs addressed to them, and sing them to tunes of her own composing; and her native wood notes wild were sweet and touching.

Her father always exclaimed against female acquirements, and was glad that his wife's indolence and ill health made her not trouble herself about them. She had besides another reason, she did not wish to have a fine tall girl brought forward into notice as her daughter; she still expected to recover, and figure away in the gay world. Her husband was very tyrannical and passionate; indeed so very easily irritated when inebriated, that Mary was continually in dread lest he should frighten her mother to death; her sickness called forth all Mary's tenderness, and exercised her compassion so continually, that it became more than a match for self-love, and was the governing propensity of her heart through life. She was violent in her temper; but she saw her father's faults, and would weep when obliged to compare his temper with her own.—She did more; artless prayers rose to Heaven for pardon, when she was conscious of having erred; and her contrition was so exceedingly painful, that she watched diligently the first movements of anger and impatience, to save herself this cruel remorse.

Sublime ideas filled her young mind—always connected with devotional sentiments; extemporary effusions of gratitude, and rhapsodies of praise would burst often from her, when she listened to the birds, or pursued the deer. She would gaze on the moon, and ramble through the gloomy path, observing the various shapes the clouds assumed, and listen to the sea that was not far distant. The wandering spirits, which she imagined inhabited every part of nature, were her constant friends and confidants. She began to consider the Great First Cause, formed just notions of his attributes, and, in particular, dwelt on his wisdom and goodness. Could she have loved her father or mother, had they returned her affection, she would not so soon, perhaps, have sought out a new world.

Her sensibility prompted her to search for an object to love; on earth it was not to be found: her mother had often disappointed her, and the apparent partiality she shewed to her brother gave her exquisite pain—produced a kind of habitual melancholy, led her into a fondness for reading tales of woe, and made her almost realize the fictitious distress.

She had not any notion of death till a little chicken expired at her feet; and her father had a dog hung in a passion. She then concluded animals had souls, or they would not have been subjected to the caprice of man; but what was the soul of man or beast? In this style year after year rolled on, her mother still vegetating.

A little girl who attended in the nursery fell sick. Mary paid her great attention; contrary to her wish, she was sent out of the house to her mother, a poor woman, whom necessity obliged to leave her sick child while she earned her daily bread. The poor wretch, in a fit of delirium stabbed herself, and Mary saw her dead body, and heard the dismal account; and so strongly did it impress her imagination, that every night of her life the bleeding corpse presented itself to her when the first began to slumber. Tortured by it, she at last made a vow, that if she was ever mistress of a family she would herself watch over every part of it. The impression that this accident made was indelible.

As her mother grew imperceptibly worse and worse, her father, who did not understand such a lingering complaint, imagined his wife was only grown still more whimsical, and that if she could be prevailed on to exert herself, her health would soon be re-established. In general he treated her with indifference; but when her illness at all interfered with his pleasures, he expostulated in the most cruel manner, and visibly harassed the invalid. Mary would then assiduously try to turn his attention to something else; and when sent out of the room, would watch at the door, until the storm was over, for unless it was, she could not rest. Other causes also contributed to disturb her repose: her mother's luke-warm manner of performing her religious duties, filled her with anguish; and when she observed her father's vices, the unbidden tears would flow. She was miserable when beggars were driven from the gate without being relieved; if she could do it unperceived, she would give them her own breakfast, and feel gratified, when, in consequence of it, she was pinched by hunger.

She had once, or twice, told her little secrets to her mother; they were laughed at, and she determined never to do it again. In this manner was she left to reflect on her own feelings; and so strengthened were they by being meditated on, that her character early became singular and permanent. Her understanding was strong and clear, when not clouded by her feelings; but she was too much the creature of impulse, and the slave of compassion.

CHAPTER III

Near her father's house lived a poor widow, who had been brought up in affluence, but reduced to great distress by the extravagance of her husband; he had destroyed his constitution while he spent his fortune; and dying, left his wife, and five small children, to live on a very scanty pittance. The eldest daughter was for some years educated by a distant relation, a Clergyman. While she was with him a young gentleman, son to a man of property in the neighbourhood, took particular notice of her. It is true, he never talked of love; but then they played and sung in concert; drew landscapes together, and while she worked he read to her, cultivated her taste, and stole imperceptibly her heart. Just at this juncture, when smiling, unanalyzed hope made every prospect bright, and gay expectation danced in her eyes, her benefactor died. She returned to her mother—the companion of her youth forgot her, they took no more sweet counsel together. This disappointment spread a sadness over her countenance, and made it interesting. She grew fond of solitude, and her character appeared similar to Mary's, though her natural disposition was very different.

She was several years older than Mary, yet her refinement, her taste, caught her eye, and she eagerly sought her friendship: before her return she had assisted the family, which was almost reduced to the last ebb; and now she had another motive to actuate her.

As she had often occasion to send messages to Ann, her new friend, mistakes were frequently made; Ann proposed that in future they should be written ones, to obviate this difficulty, and render their intercourse more agreeable. Young people are mostly fond of scribbling; Mary had had very little instruction; but by copying her friend's letters, whose hand she admired, she soon became a proficient; a little practice made her write with tolerable correctness, and her genius gave force to it. In conversation, and in writing, when she felt, she was pathetic, tender and persuasive; and she expressed contempt with such energy, that few could stand the flash of her eyes.

As she grew more intimate with Ann, her manners were softened, and she acquired a degree of equality in her behaviour: yet still her spirits were fluctuating, and her movements rapid. She felt less pain on account of her mother's partiality to her brother, as she hoped now to experience the pleasure of being beloved; but this hope led her into new sorrows, and, as usual, paved the way for disappointment. Ann only felt gratitude; her heart was entirely engrossed by one object, and friendship could not serve as a substitute; memory officiously retraced past scenes, and unavailing wishes made time loiter.

Mary was often hurt by the involuntary indifference which these consequences produced. When her friend was all the world to her, she found she was not as necessary to her happiness; and her delicate mind could not bear to obtrude her affection, or receive love as an alms, the offspring of pity. Very frequently has she ran to her with delight, and not perceiving any thing of the same kind in Ann's countenance, she has shrunk back; and, falling from one extreme into the other, instead of a warm greeting that was just slipping from her tongue, her expressions seemed to be dictated by the most chilling insensibility.

She would then imagine that she looked sickly or unhappy, and then all her tenderness would return like a torrent, and bear away all reflection. In this manner was her sensibility called forth, and exercised, by her mother's illness, her friend's misfortunes, and her own unsettled mind.

CHAPTER IV

Near to her father's house was a range of mountains; some of them were, literally speaking, cloud-capt, for on them clouds continually rested, and gave grandeur to the prospect; and down many of their sides the little bubbling cascades ran till they swelled a beautiful river. Through the straggling trees and bushes the wind whistled, and on them the birds sung, particularly the robins; they also found shelter in the ivy of an old castle, a haunted one, as the story went; it was situated on the brow of one of the mountains, and commanded a view of the sea. This castle had been inhabited by some of her ancestors; and many tales had the old house-keeper told her of the worthies who had resided there.

When her mother frowned, and her friend looked cool, she would steal to this retirement, where human foot seldom trod—gaze on the sea, observe the grey clouds, or listen to the wind which struggled to free itself from the only thing that impeded its course. When more cheerful, she admired the various dispositions of light and shade, the beautiful tints the gleams of sunshine gave to the distant hills; then she rejoiced in existence, and darted into futurity.

One way home was through the cavity of a rock covered with a thin layer of earth, just sufficient to afford nourishment to a few stunted shrubs and wild plants, which grew on its sides, and nodded over the summit. A clear stream broke out of it, and ran amongst the pieces of rocks fallen into it. Here twilight always reigned—it seemed the Temple of Solitude; yet, paradoxical as the assertion may appear, when the foot sounded on the rock, it terrified the intruder, and inspired a strange feeling, as if the rightful sovereign was dislodged. In this retreat she read Thomson's Seasons, Young's Night-Thoughts, and Paradise Lost.

At a little distance from it were the huts of a few poor fishermen, who supported their numerous children by their precarious labour. In these little huts she frequently rested, and denied herself every childish gratification, in order to relieve the necessities of the inhabitants. Her heart yearned for them, and would dance with joy when she had relieved their wants, or afforded them pleasure.

In these pursuits she learned the luxury of doing good; and the sweet tears of benevolence frequently moistened her eyes, and gave them a sparkle which, exclusive of that, they had not; on the contrary, they were rather fixed, and would never have been observed if her soul had not animated them. They were not at all like those brilliant ones which look like polished diamonds, and dart from every superfice, giving more light to the beholders than they receive themselves.

Her benevolence, indeed, knew no bounds; the distress of others carried her out of herself; and she rested not till she had relieved or comforted them. The warmth of her compassion often made her so diligent, that many things occurred to her, which might have escaped a less interested observer.

In like manner, she entered with such spirit into whatever she read, and the emotions thereby raised were so strong, that it soon became a part of her mind.

Enthusiastic sentiments of devotion at this period actuated her; her Creator was almost apparent to her senses in his works; but they were mostly the grand or solemn features of Nature which she delighted to contemplate. She would stand and behold the waves rolling, and think of the voice that could still the tumultuous deep.

These propensities gave the colour to her mind, before the passions began to exercise their tyrannic sway, and particularly pointed out those which the soil would have a tendency to nurse.

Years after, when wandering through the same scenes, her imagination has strayed back, to trace the first placid sentiments they inspired, and she would earnestly desire to regain the same peaceful tranquillity.

Many nights she sat up, if I may be allowed the expression, conversing with the Author of Nature, making verses, and singing hymns of her own composing. She considered also, and tried to discern what end her various faculties were destined to pursue; and had a glimpse of a truth, which afterwards more fully unfolded itself.

She thought that only an infinite being could fill the human soul, and that when other objects were followed as a means of happiness, the delusion led to misery, the consequence of disappointment. Under the influence of ardent affections, how often has she forgot this conviction, and as often returned to it again, when it struck her with redoubled force. Often did she taste unmixed delight; her joys, her ecstacies arose from genius.

She was now fifteen, and she wished to receive the holy sacrament; and perusing the scriptures, and discussing some points of doctrine which puzzled her, she would sit up half the night, her favourite time for employing her mind; she too plainly perceived that she saw through a glass darkly; and that the bounds set to stop our intellectual researches, is one of the trials of a probationary state.

But her affections were roused by the display of divine mercy; and she eagerly desired to commemorate the dying love of her great benefactor. The night before the important day, when she was to take on herself her baptismal vow, she could not go to bed; the sun broke in on her meditations, and found her not exhausted by her watching.

The orient pearls were strewed around—she hailed the morn, and sung with wild delight, Glory to God on high, good will towards men. She was indeed so much affected when she joined in the prayer for her eternal preservation, that she could hardly conceal her violent emotions; and the recollection never failed to wake her dormant piety when earthly passions made it grow languid.

These various movements of her mind were not commented on, nor were the luxuriant shoots restrained by culture. The servants and the poor adored her.

In order to be enabled to gratify herself in the highest degree, she practiced the most rigid oeconomy, and had such power over her appetites and whims, that without any great effort she conquered them so entirely, that when her understanding or affections had an object, she almost forgot she had a body which required nourishment.

This habit of thinking, this kind of absorption, gave strength to the passions.

We will now enter on the more active field of life.

CHAPTER V

A few months after Mary was turned of seventeen, her brother was attacked by a violent fever, and died before his father could reach the school.

She was now an heiress, and her mother began to think her of consequence, and did not call her the child. Proper masters were sent for; she was taught to dance, and an extraordinary master procured to perfect her in that most necessary of all accomplishments.

A part of the estate she was to inherit had been litigated, and the heir of the person who still carried on a Chancery suit, was only two years younger than our heroine. The fathers, spite of the dispute, frequently met, and, in order to settle it amicably, they one day, over a bottle, determined to quash it by a marriage, and, by uniting the two estates, to preclude all farther enquiries into the merits of their different claims.

While this important matter was settling, Mary was otherwise employed. Ann's mother's resources were failing; and the ghastly phantom, poverty, made hasty strides to catch them in his clutches. Ann had not fortitude enough to brave such accumulated misery; besides, the canker-worm was lodged in her heart, and preyed on her health. She denied herself every little comfort; things that would be no sacrifice when a person is well, are absolutely necessary to alleviate bodily pain, and support the animal functions.

There were many elegant amusements, that she had acquired a relish for, which might have taken her mind off from its most destructive bent; but these her indigence would not allow her to enjoy: forced then, by way of relaxation, to play the tunes her lover admired, and handle the pencil he taught her to hold, no wonder his image floated on her imagination, and that taste invigorated love.

Poverty, and all its inelegant attendants, were in her mother's abode; and she, though a good sort of a woman, was not calculated to banish, by her trivial, uninteresting chat, the delirium in which her daughter was lost.

This ill-fated love had given a bewitching softness to her manners, a delicacy so truly feminine, that a man of any feeling could not behold her without wishing to chase her sorrows away. She was timid and irresolute, and rather fond of dissipation; grief only had power to make her reflect.

In every thing it was not the great, but the beautiful, or the pretty, that caught her attention. And in composition, the polish of style, and harmony of numbers, interested her much more than the flights of genius, or abstracted speculations.

She often wondered at the books Mary chose, who, though she had a lively imagination, would frequently study authors whose works were addressed to the understanding. This liking taught her to arrange her thoughts, and argue with herself, even when under the influence of the most violent passions.

Ann's misfortunes and ill health were strong ties to bind Mary to her; she wished so continually to have a home to receive her in, that it drove every other desire out of her mind; and, dwelling on the tender schemes which compassion and friendship dictated, she longed most ardently to put them in practice.

Fondly as she loved her friend, she did not forget her mother, whose decline was so imperceptible, that they were not aware of her approaching dissolution. The physician, however, observing the most alarming symptoms; her husband was apprised of her immediate danger; and then first mentioned to her his designs with respect to his daughter.

She approved of them; Mary was sent for; she was not at home; she had rambled to visit Ann, and found her in an hysteric fit. The landlord of her little farm had sent his agent for the rent, which had long been due to him; and he threatened to seize the stock that still remained, and turn them out, if they did not very shortly discharge the arrears.

As this man made a private fortune by harassing the tenants of the person to whom he was deputy, little was to be expected from his forbearance.

All this was told to Mary—and the mother added, she had many other creditors who would, in all probability, take the alarm, and snatch from them all that had been saved out of the wreck. "I could bear all," she cried; "but what will become of my children? Of this child," pointing to the fainting Ann, "whose constitution is already undermined by care and grief—where will she go?"—Mary's heart ceased to beat while she asked the question—She attempted to speak; but the inarticulate sounds died away. Before she had recovered herself, her father called himself to enquire for her; and desired her instantly to accompany him home.

Engrossed by the scene of misery she had been witness to, she walked silently by his side, when he roused her out of her reverie by telling her that in all likelihood her mother had not many hours to live; and before she could return him any answer, informed her that they had both determined to marry her to Charles, his friend's son; he added, the ceremony was to be performed directly, that her mother might be witness of it; for such a desire she had expressed with childish eagerness.

Overwhelmed by this intelligence, Mary rolled her eyes about, then, with a vacant stare, fixed them on her father's face; but they were no longer a sense; they conveyed no ideas to the brain. As she drew near the house, her wonted presence of mind returned: after this suspension of thought, a thousand darted into her mind,—her dying mother,—her friend's miserable situation,—and an extreme horror at taking—at being forced to take, such a hasty step; but she did not feel the disgust, the reluctance, which arises from a prior attachment.

She loved Ann better than any one in the world—to snatch her from the very jaws of destruction—she would have encountered a lion. To have this friend constantly with her; to make her mind easy with respect to her family, would it not be superlative bliss?

Full of these thoughts she entered her mother's chamber, but they then fled at the sight of a dying parent. She went to her, took her hand; it feebly pressed her's. "My child," said the languid mother: the words reached her heart; she had seldom heard them pronounced with accents denoting affection; "My child, I have not always treated you with kindness—God forgive me! do you?"—Mary's tears strayed in a disregarded stream; on her bosom the big drops fell, but did not relieve the fluttering tenant. "I forgive you!" said she, in a tone of astonishment.

The clergyman came in to read the service for the sick, and afterwards the marriage ceremony was performed. Mary stood like a statue of Despair, and pronounced the awful vow without thinking of it; and then ran to support her mother, who expired the same night in her arms.

Her husband set off for the continent the same day, with a tutor, to finish his studies at one of the foreign universities.

Ann was sent for to console her, not on account of the departure of her new relation, a boy she seldom took any notice of, but to reconcile her to her fate; besides, it was necessary she should have a female companion, and there was not any maiden aunt in the family, or cousin of the same class.

CHAPTER VI

Mary was allowed to pay the rent which gave her so much uneasiness, and she exerted every nerve to prevail on her father effectually to succour the family; but the utmost she could obtain was a small sum very inadequate to the purpose, to enable the poor woman to carry into execution a little scheme of industry near the metropolis.

Her intention of leaving that part of the country, had much more weight with him, than Mary's arguments, drawn from motives of philanthropy and friendship; this was a language he did not understand; expressive of occult qualities he never thought of, as they could not be seen or felt.

After the departure of her mother, Ann still continued to languish, though she had a nurse who was entirely engrossed by the desire of amusing her. Had her health been re-established, the time would have passed in a tranquil, improving manner.

During the year of mourning they lived in retirement; music, drawing, and reading, filled up the time; and Mary's taste and judgment were both improved by contracting a habit of observation, and permitting the simple beauties of Nature to occupy her thoughts.

She had a wonderful quickness in discerning distinctions and combining ideas, that at the first glance did not appear to be similar. But these various pursuits did not banish all her cares, or carry off all her constitutional black bile. Before she enjoyed Ann's society, she imagined it would have made her completely happy: she was disappointed, and yet knew not what to complain of.

As her friend could not accompany her in her walks, and wished to be alone, for a very obvious reason, she would return to her old haunts, retrace her anticipated pleasures—and wonder how they changed their colour in possession, and proved so futile.

She had not yet found the companion she looked for. Ann and she were not congenial minds, nor did she contribute to her comfort in the degree she expected. She shielded her from poverty; but this was only a negative blessing; when under the pressure it was very grievous, and still more so were the apprehensions; but when exempt from them, she was not contented.

Such is human nature, its laws were not to be inverted to gratify our heroine, and stop the progress of her understanding, happiness only flourished in paradise—we cannot taste and live.

Another year passed away with increasing apprehensions. Ann had a hectic cough, and many unfavourable prognostics: Mary then forgot every thing but the fear of losing her, and even imagined that her recovery would have made her happy.

Her anxiety led her to study physic, and for some time she only read books of that cast; and this knowledge, literally speaking, ended in vanity and vexation of spirit, as it enabled her to foresee what she could not prevent.

As her mind expanded, her marriage appeared a dreadful misfortune; she was sometimes reminded of the heavy yoke, and bitter was the recollection!

In one thing there seemed to be a sympathy between them, for she wrote formal answers to his as formal letters. An extreme dislike took root in her mind; the found of his name made her turn sick; but she forgot all, listening to Ann's cough, and supporting her languid frame. She would then catch her to her bosom with convulsive eagerness, as if to save her from sinking into an opening grave.

CHAPTER VII

It was the will of Providence that Mary should experience almost every species of sorrow. Her father was thrown from his horse, when his blood was in a very inflammatory state, and the bruises were very dangerous; his recovery was not expected by the physical tribe.

Terrified at seeing him so near death, and yet so ill prepared for it, his daughter sat by his bed, oppressed by the keenest anguish, which her piety increased.

Her grief had nothing selfish in it; he was not a friend or protector; but he was her father, an unhappy wretch, going into eternity, depraved and thoughtless. Could a life of sensuality be a preparation for a peaceful death? Thus meditating, she passed the still midnight hour by his bedside.

The nurse fell asleep, nor did a violent thunder storm interrupt her repose, though it made the night appear still more terrific to Mary. Her father's unequal breathing alarmed her, when she heard a long drawn breath, she feared it was his last, and watching for another, a dreadful peal of thunder struck her ears. Considering the separation of the soul and body, this night seemed sadly solemn, and the hours long.

Death is indeed a king of terrors when he attacks the vicious man! The compassionate heart finds not any comfort; but dreads an eternal separation. No transporting greetings are anticipated, when the survivors also shall have finished their course; but all is black!—the grave may truly be said to receive the departed—this is the sting of death!

Night after night Mary watched, and this excessive fatigue impaired her own health, but had a worse effect on Ann; though she constantly went to bed, she could not rest; a number of uneasy thoughts obtruded themselves; and apprehensions about Mary, whom she loved as well as her exhausted heart could love, harassed her mind. After a sleepless, feverish night she had a violent fit of coughing, and burst a blood-vessel. The physician, who was in the house, was sent for, and when he left the patient, Mary, with an authoritative voice, insisted on knowing his real opinion. Reluctantly he gave it, that her friend was in a critical state; and if she passed the approaching winter in England, he imagined she would die in the spring; a season fatal to consumptive disorders. The spring!—Her husband was then expected.—Gracious Heaven, could she bear all this.

In a few days her father breathed his last. The horrid sensations his death occasioned were too poignant to be durable: and Ann's danger, and her own situation, made Mary deliberate what mode of conduct she should pursue. She feared this event might hasten the return of her husband, and prevent her putting into execution a plan she had determined on. It was to accompany Ann to a more salubrious climate.

CHAPTER VIII

I mentioned before, that Mary had never had any particular attachment, to give rise to the disgust that daily gained ground. Her friendship for Ann occupied her heart, and resembled a passion. She had had, indeed, several transient likings; but they did not amount to love. The society of men of genius delighted her, and improved her faculties. With beings of this class she did not often meet; it is a rare genus; her first favourites were men past the meridian of life, and of a philosophic turn.

Determined on going to the South of France, or Lisbon; she wrote to the man she had promised to obey. The physicians had said change of air was necessary for her as well as her friend. She mentioned this, and added, "Her comfort, almost her existence, depended on the recovery of the invalid she wished to attend; and that should she neglect to follow the medical advice she had received, she should never forgive herself, or those who endeavoured to prevent her." Full of her design, she wrote with more than usual freedom; and this letter was like most of her others, a transcript of her heart.

"This dear friend," she exclaimed, "I love for her agreeable qualities, and substantial virtues. Continual attention to her health, and the tender office of a nurse, have created an affection very like a maternal one—I am her only support, she leans on me—could I forsake the forsaken, and break the bruised reed—No—I would die first! I must—I will go."

She would have added, "you would very much oblige me by consenting;" but her heart revolted—and irresolutely she wrote something about wishing him happy.—"Do I not wish all the world well?" she cried, as she subscribed her name—It was blotted, the letter sealed in a hurry, and sent out of her sight; and she began to prepare for her journey.

By the return of the post she received an answer; it contained some common-place remarks on her romantic friendship, as he termed it; "But as the physicians advised change of air, he had no objection."

CHAPTER IX

There was nothing now to retard their journey; and Mary chose Lisbon rather than France, on account of its being further removed from the only person she wished not to see.

They set off accordingly for Falmouth, in their way to that city. The journey was of use to Ann, and Mary's spirits were raised by her recovered looks—She had been in despair—now she gave way to hope, and was intoxicated with it. On ship-board Ann always remained in the cabin; the sight of the water terrified her: on the contrary, Mary, after she was gone to bed, or when she fell asleep in the day, went on deck, conversed with the sailors, and surveyed the boundless expanse before her with delight. One instant she would regard the ocean, the next the beings who braved its fury. Their insensibility and want of fear, she could not name courage; their thoughtless mirth was quite of an animal kind, and their feelings as impetuous and uncertain as the element they plowed.

They had only been a week at sea when they hailed the rock of Lisbon, and the next morning anchored at the castle. After the customary visits, they were permitted to go on shore, about three miles from the city; and while one of the crew, who understood the language, went to procure them one of the ugly carriages peculiar to the country, they waited in the Irish convent, which is situated close to the Tagus.

Some of the people offered to conduct them into the church, where there was a fine organ playing; Mary followed them, but Ann preferred staying with a nun she had entered into conversation with.

One of the nuns, who had a sweet voice, was singing; Mary was struck with awe; her heart joined in the devotion; and tears of gratitude and tenderness flowed from her eyes. My Father, I thank thee! burst from her—words were inadequate to express her feelings. Silently, she surveyed the lofty dome; heard unaccustomed sounds; and saw faces, strange ones, that she could not yet greet with fraternal love.

In an unknown land, she considered that the Being she adored inhabited eternity, was ever present in unnumbered worlds. When she had not any one she loved near her, she was particularly sensible of the presence of her Almighty Friend.

The arrival of the carriage put a stop to her speculations; it was to conduct them to an hotel, fitted up for the reception of invalids. Unfortunately, before they could reach it there was a violent shower of rain; and as the wind was very high, it beat against the leather curtains, which they drew along the front of the vehicle, to shelter themselves from it; but it availed not, some of the rain forced its way, and Ann felt the effects of it, for she caught cold, spite of Mary's precautions.

As is the custom, the rest of the invalids, or lodgers, sent to enquire after their health; and as soon as Ann left her chamber, in which her complaints seldom confined her the whole day, they came in person to pay their compliments. Three fashionable females, and two gentlemen; the one a brother of the eldest of the young ladies, and the other an invalid, who came, like themselves, for the benefit of the air. They entered into conversation immediately.

People who meet in a strange country, and are all together in a house, soon get acquainted, without the formalities which attend visiting in separate houses, where they are surrounded by domestic friends. Ann was particularly delighted at meeting with agreeable society; a little hectic fever generally made her low-spirited in the morning, and lively in the evening, when she wished for company. Mary, who only thought of her, determined to cultivate their acquaintance, as she knew, that if her mind could be diverted, her body might gain strength.

They were all musical, and proposed having little concerts. One of the gentlemen played on the violin, and the other on the german-flute. The instruments were brought in, with all the eagerness that attends putting a new scheme in execution.

Mary had not said much, for she was diffident; she seldom joined in general conversations; though her quickness of penetration enabled her soon to enter into the characters of those she conversed with; and her sensibility made her desirous of pleasing every human creature. Besides, if her mind was not occupied by any particular sorrow, or study, she caught reflected pleasure, and was glad to see others happy, though their mirth did not interest her.

This day she was continually thinking of Ann's recovery, and encouraging the cheerful hopes, which though they dissipated the spirits that had been condensed by melancholy, yet made her wish to be silent. The music, more than the conversation, disturbed her reflections; but not at first. The gentleman who played on the german-flute, was a handsome, well-bred, sensible man; and his observations, if not original, were pertinent.

The other, who had not said much, began to touch the violin, and played a little Scotch ballad; he brought such a thrilling sound out of the instrument, that Mary started, and looking at him with more attention than she had done before, and saw, in a face rather ugly, strong lines of genius. His manners were awkward, that kind of awkwardness which is often found in literary men: he seemed a thinker, and delivered his opinions in elegant expressions, and musical tones of voice.

When the concert was over, they all retired to their apartments. Mary always slept with Ann, as she was subject to terrifying dreams; and frequently in the night was obliged to be supported, to avoid suffocation. They chatted about their new acquaintance in their own apartment, and, with respect to the gentlemen, differed in opinion.

CHAPTER X

Every day almost they saw their new acquaintance; and civility produced intimacy. Mary sometimes left her friend with them; while she indulged herself in viewing new modes of life, and searching out the causes which produced them. She had a metaphysical turn, which inclined her to reflect on every object that passed by her; and her mind was not like a mirror, which receives every floating image, but does not retain them: she had not any prejudices, for every opinion was examined before it was adopted.

The Roman Catholic ceremonies attracted her attention, and gave rise to conversations when they all met; and one of the gentlemen continually introduced deistical notions, when he ridiculed the pageantry they all were surprised at observing. Mary thought of both the subjects, the Romish tenets, and the deistical doubts; and though not a sceptic, thought it right to examine the evidence on which her faith was built. She read Butler's Analogy, and some other authors: and these researches made her a christian from conviction, and she learned charity, particularly with respect to sectaries; saw that apparently good and solid arguments might take their rise from different points of view; and she rejoiced to find that those she should not concur with had some reason on their side.

CHAPTER XI

When I mentioned the three ladies, I said they were fashionable women; and it was all the praise, as a faithful historian, I could bestow on them; the only thing in which they were consistent. I forgot to mention that they were all of one family, a mother, her daughter, and niece. The daughter was sent by her physician, to avoid a northerly winter; the mother, her niece, and nephew, accompanied her.

They were people of rank; but unfortunately, though of an ancient family, the title had descended to a very remote branch—a branch they took care to be intimate with; and servilely copied the Countess's airs. Their minds were shackled with a set of notions concerning propriety, the fitness of things for the world's eye, trammels which always hamper weak people. What will the world say? was the first thing that was thought of, when they intended doing any thing they had not done before. Or what would the Countess do on such an occasion? And when this question was answered, the right or wrong was discovered without the trouble of their having any idea of the matter in their own heads. This same Countess was a fine planet, and the satellites observed a most harmonic dance around her.

After this account it is scarcely necessary to add, that their minds had received very little cultivation. They were taught French, Italian, and Spanish; English was their vulgar tongue. And what did they learn? Hamlet will tell you—words—words. But let me not forget that they squalled Italian songs in the true gusto. Without having any seeds sown in their understanding, or the affections of the heart set to work, they were brought out of their nursery, or the place they were secluded in, to prevent their faces being common; like blazing stars, to captivate Lords.

They were pretty, and hurrying from one party of pleasure to another, occasioned the disorder which required change of air. The mother, if we except her being near twenty years older, was just the same creature; and these additional years only served to make her more tenaciously adhere to her habits of folly, and decide with stupid gravity, some trivial points of ceremony, as a matter of the last importance; of which she was a competent judge, from having lived in the fashionable world so long: that world to which the ignorant look up as we do to the sun.

It appears to me that every creature has some notion—or rather relish, of the sublime. Riches, and the consequent state, are the sublime of weak minds:—These images fill, nay, are too big for their narrow souls.

One afternoon, which they had engaged to spend together, Ann was so ill, that Mary was obliged to send an apology for not attending the tea-table. The apology brought them on the carpet; and the mother, with a look of solemn importance, turned to the sick man, whose name was Henry, and said;

"Though people of the first fashion are frequently at places of this kind, intimate with they know not who; yet I do not choose that my daughter, whose family is so respectable, should be intimate with any one she would blush to know elsewhere. It is only on that account, for I never suffer her to be with any one but in my company," added she, sitting more erect; and a smile of self-complacency dressed her countenance.

"I have enquired concerning these strangers, and find that the one who has the most dignity in her manners, is really a woman of fortune." "Lord, mamma, how ill she dresses:" mamma went on; "She is a romantic creature, you must not copy her, miss; yet she is an heiress of the large fortune in —shire, of which you may remember to have heard the Countess speak the night you had on the dancing-dress that was so much admired; but she is married."

She then told them the whole story as she heard it from her maid, who picked it out of Mary's servant. "She is a foolish creature, and this friend that she pays as much attention to as if she was a lady of quality, is a beggar." "Well, how strange!" cried the girls.

"She is, however, a charming creature," said her nephew. Henry sighed, and strode across the room once or twice; then took up his violin, and played the air which first struck Mary; he had often heard her praise it.

The music was uncommonly melodious, "And came stealing on the senses like the sweet south." The well-known sounds reached Mary as she sat by her friend—she listened without knowing that she did—and shed tears almost without being conscious of it. Ann soon fell asleep, as she had taken an opiate. Mary, then brooding over her fears, began to imagine she had deceived herself—Ann was still very ill; hope had beguiled many heavy hours; yet she was displeased with herself for admitting this welcome guest.—And she worked up her mind to such a degree of anxiety, that she determined, once more, to seek medical aid.

No sooner did she determine, than she ran down with a discomposed look, to enquire of the ladies who she should send for. When she entered the room she could not articulate her fears—it appeared like pronouncing Ann's sentence of death; her faultering tongue dropped some broken words, and she remained silent. The ladies wondered that a person of her sense should be so little mistress of herself; and began to administer some common-place comfort, as, that it was our duty to submit to the will of Heaven, and the like trite consolations, which Mary did not answer; but waving her hand, with an air of impatience, she exclaimed, "I cannot live without her!—I have no other friend; if I lose her, what a desart will the world be to me." "No other friend," re-echoed they, "have you not a husband?"

Mary shrunk back, and was alternately pale and red. A delicate sense of propriety prevented her replying; and recalled her bewildered reason.—Assuming, in consequence of her recollection, a more composed manner, she made the intended enquiry, and left the room. Henry's eyes followed her while the females very freely animadverted on her strange behaviour.

CHAPTER XII

The physician was sent for; his prescription afforded Ann a little temporary relief; and they again joined the circle. Unfortunately, the weather happened to be constantly wet for more than a week, and confined them to the house. Ann then found the ladies not so agreeable; when they sat whole hours together, the thread-bare topics were exhausted; and, but for cards or music, the long evenings would have been yawned away in listless indolence.

The bad weather had had as ill an effect on Henry as on Ann. He was frequently very thoughtful, or rather melancholy; this melancholy would of itself have attracted Mary's notice, if she had not found his conversation so infinitely superior to the rest of the group. When she conversed with him, all the faculties of her soul unfolded themselves; genius animated her expressive countenance and the most graceful, unaffected gestures gave energy to her discourse.

They frequently discussed very important subjects, while the rest were singing or playing cards, nor were they observed for doing so, as Henry, whom they all were pleased with, in the way of gallantry shewed them all more attention than her. Besides, as there was nothing alluring in her dress or manner, they never dreamt of her being preferred to them.

Henry was a man of learning; he had also studied mankind, and knew many of the intricacies of the human heart, from having felt the infirmities of his own. His taste was just, as it had a standard—Nature, which he observed with a critical eye. Mary could not help thinking that in his company her mind expanded, as he always went below the surface. She increased her stock of ideas, and her taste was improved.

He was also a pious man; his rational religious sentiments received warmth from his sensibility; and, except on very particular occasions, kept it in proper bounds; these sentiments had likewise formed his temper; he was gentle, and easily to be intreated. The ridiculous ceremonies they were every day witness to, led them into what are termed grave subjects, and made him explain his opinions, which, at other times, he was neither ashamed of, nor unnecessarily brought forward to notice.

CHAPTER XIII

When the weather began to clear up, Mary sometimes rode out alone, purposely to view the ruins that still remained of the earthquake: or she would ride to the banks of the Tagus, to feast her eyes with the sight of that magnificent river. At other times she would visit the churches, as she was particularly fond of seeing historical paintings.

One of these visits gave rise to the subject, and the whole party descanted on it; but as the ladies could not handle it well, they soon adverted to portraits; and talked of the attitudes and characters in which they should wish to be drawn. Mary did not fix on one—when Henry, with more apparent warmth than usual, said, "I would give the world for your picture, with the expression I have seen in your face, when you have been supporting your friend."

This delicate compliment did not gratify her vanity, but it reached her heart. She then recollected that she had once sat for her picture—for whom was it designed? For a boy! Her cheeks flushed with indignation, so strongly did she feel an emotion of contempt at having been thrown away—given in with an estate.

As Mary again gave way to hope, her mind was more disengaged; and her thoughts were employed about the objects around her.

She visited several convents, and found that solitude only eradicates some passions, to give strength to others; the most baneful ones. She saw that religion does not consist in ceremonies; and that many prayers may fall from the lips without purifying the heart.

They who imagine they can be religious without governing their tempers, or exercising benevolence in its most extensive sense, must certainly allow, that their religious duties are only practiced from selfish principles; how then can they be called good? The pattern of all goodness went about doing good. Wrapped up in themselves, the nuns only thought of inferior gratifications. And a number of intrigues were carried on to accelerate certain points on which their hearts were fixed:

Such as obtaining offices of trust or authority; or avoiding those that were servile or laborious. In short, when they could be neither wives nor mothers, they aimed at being superiors, and became the most selfish creatures in the world: the passions that were curbed gave strength to the appetites, or to those mean passions which only tend to provide for the gratification of them. Was this seclusion from the world? or did they conquer its vanities or avoid its vexations?

In these abodes the unhappy individual, who, in the first paroxysm of grief flies to them for refuge, finds too late she took a wrong step. The same warmth which determined her will make her repent; and sorrow, the rust of the mind, will never have a chance of being rubbed off by sensible conversation, or new-born affections of the heart.

She will find that those affections that have once been called forth and strengthened by exercise, are only smothered, not killed, by disappointment; and that in one form or other discontent will corrode the heart, and produce those maladies of the imagination, for which there is no specific.

The community at large Mary disliked; but pitied many of them whose private distresses she was informed of; and to pity and relieve were the same things with her.

The exercise of her various virtues gave vigor to her genius, and dignity to her mind; she was sometimes inconsiderate, and violent; but never mean or cunning.

CHAPTER XIV

The Portuguese are certainly the most uncivilized nation in Europe. Dr. Johnson would have said, "They have the least mind.". And can such serve their Creator in spirit and in truth? No, the gross ritual of Romish ceremonies is all they can comprehend: they can do penance, but not conquer their revenge, or lust. Religion, or love, has never humanized their hearts; they want the vital part; the mere body worships. Taste is unknown; Gothic finery, and unnatural decorations, which they term ornaments, are conspicuous in their churches and dress. Reverence for mental excellence is only to be found in a polished nation.

Could the contemplation of such a people gratify Mary's heart? No: she turned disgusted from the prospects—turned to a man of refinement. Henry had been some time ill and low-spirited; Mary would have been attentive to any one in that situation; but to him she was particularly so; she thought herself bound in gratitude, on account of his constant endeavours to amuse Ann, and prevent her dwelling on the dreary prospect before her, which sometimes she could not help anticipating with a kind of quiet despair.

She found some excuse for going more frequently into the room they all met in; nay, she avowed her desire to amuse him: offered to read to him, and tried to draw him into amusing conversations; and when she was full of these little schemes, she looked at him with a degree of tenderness that she was not conscious of. This divided attention was of use to her, and prevented her continually thinking of Ann, whose fluctuating disorder often gave rise to false hopes.

A trifling thing occurred now which occasioned Mary some uneasiness. Her maid, a well-looking girl, had captivated the clerk of a neighbouring compting-house. As the match was an advantageous one, Mary could not raise any objection to it, though at this juncture it was very disagreeable to her to have a stranger about her person. However, the girl consented to delay the marriage, as she had some affection for her mistress; and, besides, looked forward to Ann's death as a time of harvest.

Henry's illness was not alarming, it was rather pleasing, as it gave Mary an excuse to herself for shewing him how much she was interested about him; and giving little artless proofs of affection, which the purity of her heart made her never wish to restrain.

The only visible return he made was not obvious to common observers. He would sometimes fix his eyes on her, and take them off with a sigh that was coughed away; or when he was leisurely walking into the room, and did not expect to see her, he would quicken his steps, and come up to her with eagerness to ask some trivial question. In the same style, he would try to detain her when he had nothing to say—or said nothing.

Ann did not take notice of either his or Mary's behaviour, nor did she suspect that he was a favourite, on any other account than his appearing neither well nor happy. She had often seen that when a person was unfortunate, Mary's pity might easily be mistaken for love, and, indeed, it was a temporary sensation of that kind. Such it was—why it was so, let others define, I cannot argue against instincts. As reason is cultivated in man, they are supposed to grow weaker, and this may have given rise to the assertion, "That as judgment improves, genius evaporates."

CHAPTER XV

One morning they set out to visit the aqueduct; though the day was very fine when they left home, a very heavy shower fell before they reached it; they lengthened their ride, the clouds dispersed, and the sun came from behind them uncommonly bright.

Mary would fain have persuaded Ann not to have left the carriage; but she was in spirits, and obviated all her objections, and insisted on walking, tho' the ground was damp. But her strength was not equal to her spirits; she was soon obliged to return to the carriage so much fatigued, that she fainted, and remained insensible a long time.

Henry would have supported her; but Mary would not permit him; her recollection was instantaneous, and she feared sitting on the damp ground might do him a material injury: she was on that account positive, though the company did not guess the cause of her being so. As to herself, she did not fear bodily pain; and, when her mind was agitated, she could endure the greatest fatigue without appearing sensible of it.

When Ann recovered, they returned slowly home; she was carried to bed, and the next morning Mary thought she observed a visible change for the worse. The physician was sent for, who pronounced her to be in the most imminent danger.

All Mary's former fears now returned like a torrent, and carried every other care away; she even added to her present anguish by upbraiding herself for her late tranquillity—it haunted her in the form of a crime.

The disorder made the most rapid advances—there was no hope!—Bereft of it, Mary again was tranquil; but it was a very different kind of tranquillity. She stood to brave the approaching storm, conscious she only could be overwhelmed by it.

She did not think of Henry, or if her thoughts glanced towards him, it was only to find fault with herself for suffering a thought to have strayed from Ann.—Ann!—this dear friend was soon torn from her—she died suddenly as Mary was assisting her to walk across the room.—The first string was severed from her heart—and this "slow, sudden-death" disturbed her reasoning faculties; she seemed stunned by it; unable to reflect, or even to feel her misery.

The body was stolen out of the house the second night, and Mary refused to see her former companions. She desired her maid to conclude her marriage, and request her intended husband to inform her when the first merchantman was to leave the port, as the packet had just sailed, and she determined not to stay in that hated place any longer than was absolutely necessary.

She then sent to request the ladies to visit her; she wished to avoid a parade of grief—her sorrows were her own, and appeared to her not to admit of increase or softening. She was right; the sight of them did not affect her, or turn the stream of her sullen sorrow; the black wave rolled along in the same course, it was equal to her where she cast her eyes; all was impenetrable gloom.

CHAPTER XVI

Soon after the ladies left her, she received a message from Henry, requesting, as she saw company, to be permitted to visit her: she consented, and he entered immediately, with an unassured pace. She ran eagerly up to him—saw the tear trembling in his eye, and his countenance softened by the tenderest compassion; the hand which pressed hers seemed that of a fellow-creature. She burst into tears; and, unable to restrain them, she hid her face with both her hands; these tears relieved her, (she had before had a difficulty in breathing,) and she sat down by him more composed than she had appeared since Ann's death; but her conversation was incoherent.

She called herself "a poor disconsolate creature!"—"Mine is a selfish grief," she exclaimed—"Yet; Heaven is my witness, I do not wish her back now she has reached those peaceful mansions, where the weary rest. Her pure spirit is happy; but what a wretch am I!"

Henry forgot his cautious reserve. "Would you allow me to call you friend?" said he in a hesitating voice. "I feel, dear girl, the tendered interest in whatever concerns thee." His eyes spoke the rest. They were both silent a few moments; then Henry resumed the conversation. "I have also been acquainted with grief! I mourn the loss of a woman who was not worthy of my regard. Let me give thee some account of the man who now solicits thy friendship; and who, from motives of the purest benevolence, wishes to give comfort to thy wounded heart."

"I have myself," said he, mournfully, "shaken hands with happiness, and am dead to the world; I wait patiently for my dissolution; but, for thee, Mary, there may be many bright days in store."

"Impossible," replied she, in a peevish tone, as if he had insulted her by the supposition; her feelings were so much in unison with his, that she was in love with misery.

He smiled at her impatience, and went on. "My father died before I knew him, and my mother was so attached to my eldest brother, that she took very little pains to fit me for the profession to which I was destined: and, may I tell thee, I left my family, and, in many different stations, rambled about the world; saw mankind in every rank of life; and, in order to be independent, exerted those talents Nature has given me: these exertions improved my understanding; and the miseries I was witness to, gave a keener edge to my sensibility. My constitution is naturally weak; and, perhaps, two or three lingering disorders in my youth, first gave me a habit of reflecting, and enabled me to obtain some dominion over my passions. At least," added he, stifling a sigh, "over the violent ones, though I fear, refinement and reflection only renders the tender ones more tyrannic.

"I have told you already I have been in love, and disappointed—the object is now no more; let her faults sleep with her! Yet this passion has pervaded my whole soul, and mixed itself with all my affections and pursuits.—I am not peacefully indifferent; yet it is only to my violin I tell the sorrows I now confide with thee. The object I loved forfeited my esteem; yet, true to the sentiment, my fancy has too frequently delighted to form a creature that I could love, that could convey to my soul sensations which the gross part of mankind have not any conception of."

He stopped, as Mary seemed lost in thought; but as she was still in a listening attitude, continued his little narrative. "I kept up an irregular correspondence with my mother; my brother's extravagance and ingratitude had almost broken her heart, and made her feel something like a pang of remorse, on account of her behaviour to me. I hastened to comfort her—and was a comfort to her.

"My declining health prevented my taking orders, as I had intended; but I with warmth entered into literary pursuits; perhaps my heart, not having an object, made me embrace the substitute with more eagerness. But, do not imagine I have always been a die-away swain. No: I have frequented the cheerful haunts of men, and wit!—enchanting wit! has made many moments fly free from care. I am too fond of the elegant arts; and woman—lovely woman! thou hast charmed me, though, perhaps, it would not be easy to find one to whom my reason would allow me to be constant.

"I have now only to tell you, that my mother insisted on my spending this winter in a warmer climate; and I fixed on Lisbon, as I had before visited the Continent." He then looked Mary full in the face; and, with the most insinuating accents, asked "if he might hope for her friendship? If she would rely on him as if he was her father; and that the tenderest father could not more anxiously interest himself in the fate of a darling child, than he did in her's."

Such a crowd of thoughts all at once rushed into Mary's mind, that she in vain attempted to express the sentiments which were most predominant. Her heart longed to receive a new guest; there was a void in it: accustomed to have some one to love, she was alone, and comfortless, if not engrossed by a particular affection.

Henry saw her distress, and not to increase it, left the room. He had exerted himself to turn her thoughts into a new channel, and had succeeded; she thought of him till she began to chide herself for defrauding the dead, and, determining to grieve for Ann, she dwelt on Henry's misfortunes and ill health; and the interest he took in her fate was a balm to her sick mind. She did not reason on the subject; but she felt he was attached to her: lost in this delirium, she never asked herself what kind of an affection she had for him, or what it tended to; nor did she know that love and friendship are very distinct; she thought with rapture, that there was one person in the world who had an affection for her, and that person she admired—had a friendship for.

He had called her his dear girl; the words might have fallen from him by accident; but they did not fall to the ground. My child! His child, what an association of ideas! If I had had a father, such a father!—She could not dwell on the thoughts, the wishes which obtruded themselves. Her mind was unhinged, and passion unperceived filled her whole soul. Lost, in waking dreams, she considered and reconsidered Henry's account of himself; till she actually thought she would tell Ann—a bitter recollection then roused her out of her reverie; and aloud she begged forgiveness of her.

By these kind of conflicts the day was lengthened; and when she went to bed, the night passed away in feverish slumbers; though they did not refresh her, she was spared the labour of thinking, of restraining her imagination; it sported uncontrouled; but took its colour from her waking train of thoughts. One instant she was supporting her dying mother; then Ann was breathing her last, and Henry was comforting her.

The unwelcome light visited her languid eyes; yet, I must tell the truth, she thought she should see Henry, and this hope set her spirits in motion: but they were quickly depressed by her maid, who came to tell her that she had heard of a vessel on board of which she could be accommodated, and that there was to be another female passenger on board, a vulgar one; but perhaps she would be more useful on that account—Mary did not want a companion.

As she had given orders for her passage to be engaged in the first vessel that sailed, she could not now retract; and must prepare for the lonely voyage, as the Captain intended taking advantage of the first fair wind. She had too much strength of mind to waver in her determination but to determine wrung her very heart, opened all her old wounds, and made them bleed afresh. What was she to do? where go? Could she set a seal to a hasty vow, and tell a deliberate lie; promise to love one man, when the image of another was ever present to her—her soul revolted. "I might gain the applause of the world by such mock heroism; but should I not forfeit my own? forfeit thine, my father!"

There is a solemnity in the shortest ejaculation, which, for a while, stills the tumult of passion. Mary's mind had been thrown off its poise; her devotion had been, perhaps, more fervent for some time past; but less regular. She forgot that happiness was not to be found on earth, and built a terrestrial paradise liable to be destroyed by the first serious thought: when, she reasoned she became inexpressibly sad, to render life bearable she gave way to fancy—this was madness.

In a few days she must again go to sea; the weather was very tempestuous—what of that, the tempest in her soul rendered every other trifling—it was not the contending elements, but herself she feared!

CHAPTER XVII

In order to gain strength to support the expected interview, she went out in a carriage. The day was fine; but all nature was to her a universal blank; she could neither enjoy it, nor weep that she could not. She passed by the ruins of an old monastery on a very high hill she got out to walk amongst the ruins; the wind blew violently, she did not avoid its fury, on the contrary, wildly bid it blow on, and seemed glad to contend with it, or rather walk against it. Exhausted she returned to the carriage was soon at home, and in the old room.

Henry started at the sight of her altered appearance; the day before her complexion had been of the most pallid hue; but now her cheeks were flushed, and her eyes enlivened with a false vivacity, an unusual fire. He was not well, his illness was apparent in his countenance, and he owned he had not closed his eyes all night; this roused her dormant tenderness, she forgot they were so soon to part—engrossed by the present happiness of seeing, of hearing him.

Once or twice she essayed to tell him that she was, in a few days, to depart; but she could not; she was irresolute; it will do to-morrow; should the wind change they could not sail in such a hurry; thus she thought, and insensibly grew more calm. The Ladies prevailed on her to spend the evening with them; but she retired very early to rest, and sat on the side of her bed several hours, then threw herself on it, and waited for the dreaded to-morrow.

CHAPTER XVIII

The ladies heard that her servant was to be married that day, and that she was to sail in the vessel which was then clearing out at the Custom-house. Henry heard, but did not make any remarks; and Mary called up all her fortitude to support her, and enable her to hide from the females her internal struggles. She durst not encounter Henry's glances when she found he had been informed of her intention; and, trying to draw a veil over her wretched state of mind, she talked incessantly, she knew not what; flashes of wit burst from her, and when she began to laugh she could not stop herself.

Henry smiled at some of her sallies, and looked at her with such benignity and compassion, that he recalled her scattered thoughts; and, the ladies going to dress for dinner, they were left alone; and remained silent a few moments: after the noisy conversation it appeared solemn. Henry began. "You are going, Mary, and going by yourself; your mind is not in a state to be left to its own operations—yet I cannot, dissuade you; if I attempted to do it, I should ill deserve the title I wish to merit. I only think of your happiness; could I obey the strongest impulse of my heart, I should accompany thee to England; but such a step might endanger your future peace."

Mary, then, with all the frankness which marked her character, explained her situation to him and mentioned her fatal tie with such disgust that he trembled for her. "I cannot see him; he is not the man formed for me to love!" Her delicacy did not restrain her, for her dislike to her husband had taken root in her mind long before she knew Henry. Did she not fix on Lisbon rather than France on purpose to avoid him? and if Ann had been in tolerable health she would have flown with her to some remote corner to have escaped from him.

"I intend," said Henry, "to follow you in the next packet; where shall I hear of your health?" "Oh! let me hear of thine," replied Mary. "I am well, very well; but thou art very ill—thy health is in the most precarious state." She then mentioned her intention of going to Ann's relations. "I am her representative, I have duties to fulfil for her: during my voyage I have time enough for reflection; though I think I have already determined."

"Be not too hasty, my child," interrupted Henry; "far be it from me to persuade thee to do violence to thy feelings—but consider that all thy future life may probably take its colour from thy present mode of conduct. Our affections as well as our sentiments are fluctuating; you will not perhaps always either think or feel as you do at present: the object you now shun may appear in a different light." He paused. "In advising thee in this style, I have only thy good at heart, Mary."

She only answered to expostulate. "My affections are involuntary—yet they can only be fixed by reflection, and when they are they make quite a part of my soul, are interwoven in it, animate my actions, and form my taste: certain qualities are calculated to call forth my sympathies, and make me all I am capable of being. The governing affection gives its stamp to the rest—because I am capable of loving one, I have that kind of charity to all my fellow-creatures which is not easily provoked. Milton has asserted, That earthly love is the scale by which to heavenly we may ascend."

She went on with eagerness. "My opinions on some subjects are not wavering; my pursuit through life has ever been the same: in solitude were my sentiments formed; they are indelible, and nothing can efface them but death—No, death itself cannot efface them, or my soul must be created afresh, and not improved. Yet a little while am I parted from my Ann—I could not exist without the hope of seeing her again—I could not bear to think that time could wear away an affection that was founded on what is not liable to perish; you might as well attempt to persuade me that my soul is matter, and that its feelings arose from certain modifications of it."

"Dear enthusiastic creature," whispered Henry, "how you steal into my soul." She still continued. "The same turn of mind which leads me to adore the Author of all Perfection—which leads me to conclude that he only can fill my soul; forces me to admire the faint image-the shadows of his attributes here below; and my imagination gives still bolder strokes to them. I knew I am in some degree under the influence of a delusion—but does not this strong delusion prove that I myself 'am of subtiler essence than the trodden clod' these flights of the imagination point to futurity; I cannot banish them. Every cause in nature produces an effect; and am I an exception to the general rule? have I desires implanted in me only to make me miserable? will they never be gratified? shall I never be happy? My feelings do not accord with the notion of solitary happiness. In a state of bliss, it will be the society of beings we can love, without the alloy that earthly infirmities mix with our best affections, that will constitute great part of our happiness.

"With these notions can I conform to the maxims of worldly wisdom? can I listen to the cold dictates of worldly prudence and bid my tumultuous passions cease to vex me, be still, find content in grovelling pursuits, and the admiration of the misjudging crowd, when it is only one I wish to please—one who could be all the world to me. Argue not with me, I am bound by human ties; but did my spirit ever promise to love, or could I consider when forced to bind myself—to take a vow, that at the awful day of judgment I must give an account of. My conscience does not smite me, and that Being who is greater than the internal monitor, may approve of what the world condemns; sensible that in Him I live, could I brave His presence, or hope in solitude to find peace, if I acted contrary to conviction, that the world might approve of my conduct—what could the world give to compensate for my own esteem? it is ever hostile and armed against the feeling heart!

"Riches and honours await me, and the cold moralist might desire me to sit down and enjoy them—I cannot conquer my feelings, and till I do, what are these baubles to me? you may tell me I follow a fleeting good, an ignis fatuus; but this chase, these struggles prepare me for eternity—when I no longer see through a glass darkly I shall not reason about, but feel in what happiness consists."

Henry had not attempted to interrupt her; he saw she was determined, and that these sentiments were not the effusion of the moment, but well digested ones, the result of strong affections, a high sense of honour, and respect for the source of all virtue and truth. He was startled, if not entirely convinced by her arguments; indeed her voice, her gestures were all persuasive.

Some one now entered the room; he looked an answer to her long harangue; it was fortunate for him, or he might have been led to say what in a cooler moment he had determined to conceal; but were words necessary to reveal it? He wished not to influence her conduct—vain precaution; she knew she was beloved; and could she forget that such a man loved her, or rest satisfied with any inferior gratification. When passion first enters the heart, it is only a return of affection that is sought after, and every other remembrance and wish is blotted out.

CHAPTER XIX

Two days passed away without any particular conversation; Henry, trying to be indifferent, or to appear so, was more assiduous than ever. The conflict was too violent for his present state of health; the spirit was willing, but the body suffered; he lost his appetite, and looked wretchedly; his spirits were calmly low—the world seemed to fade away—what was that world to him that Mary did not inhabit; she lived not for him.

He was mistaken; his affection was her only support; without this dear prop she had sunk into the grave of her lost—long-loved friend;—his attention snatched her from despair. Inscrutable are the ways of Heaven!

The third day Mary was desired to prepare herself; for if the wind continued in the same point, they should set sail the next evening. She tried to prepare her mind, and her efforts were not useless she appeared less agitated than could have been expected, and talked of her voyage with composure. On great occasions she was generally calm and collected, her resolution would brace her unstrung nerves; but after the victory she had no triumph; she would sink into a state of moping melancholy, and feel ten-fold misery when the heroic enthusiasm was over.

The morning of the day fixed on for her departure she was alone with Henry only a few moments, and an awkward kind of formality made them slip away without their having said much to each other. Henry was afraid to discover his passion, or give any other name to his regard but friendship; yet his anxious solicitude for her welfare was ever breaking out-while she as artlessly expressed again and again, her fears with respect to his declining health.

"We shall soon meet," said he, with a faint smile; Mary smiled too; she caught the sickly beam; it was still fainter by being reflected, and not knowing what she wished to do, started up and left the room. When she was alone she regretted she had left him so precipitately. "The few precious moments I have thus thrown away may never return," she thought-the reflection led to misery.

She waited for, nay, almost wished for the summons to depart. She could not avoid spending the intermediate time with the ladies and Henry; and the trivial conversations she was obliged to bear a part in harassed her more than can be well conceived.

The summons came, and the whole party attended her to the vessel. For a while the remembrance of Ann banished her regret at parting with Henry, though his pale figure pressed on her sight; it may seem a paradox, but he was more present to her when she sailed; her tears then were all his own.

"My poor Ann!" thought Mary, "along this road we came, and near this spot you called me your guardian angel—and now I leave thee here! ah! no, I do not—thy spirit is not confined to its mouldering tenement! Tell me, thou soul of her I love, tell me, ah! whither art thou fled?" Ann occupied her until they reached the ship.

The anchor was weighed. Nothing can be more irksome than waiting to say farewel. As the day was serene, they accompanied her a little way, and then got into the boat; Henry was the last; he pressed her hand, it had not any life in it; she leaned over the side of the ship without looking at the boat, till it was so far distant, that she could not see the countenances of those that were in it: a mist spread itself over her sight—she longed to exchange one look—tried to recollect the last;—the universe contained no being but Henry!—The grief of parting with him had swept all others clean away. Her eyes followed the keel of the boat, and when she could no longer perceive its traces: she looked round on the wide waste of waters, thought of the precious moments which had been stolen from the waste of murdered time.

She then descended into the cabin, regardless of the surrounding beauties of nature, and throwing herself on her bed in the little hole which was called the state-room—she wished to forget her existence. On this bed she remained two days, listening to the dashing waves, unable to close her eyes. A small taper made the darkness visible; and the third night, by its glimmering light, she wrote the following fragment.

"Poor solitary wretch that I am; here alone do I listen to the whistling winds and dashing waves;—on no human support can I rest—when not lost to hope I found pleasure in the society of those rough beings; but now they appear not like my fellow creatures; no social ties draw me to them. How long, how dreary has this day been; yet I scarcely wish it over—for what will to-morrow bring—to-morrow, and to-morrow will only be marked with unvaried characters of wretchedness.—Yet surely, I am not alone!"

Her moistened eyes were lifted up to heaven; a crowd of thoughts darted into her mind, and pressing her hand against her forehead, as if to bear the intellectual weight, she tried, but tried in vain, to arrange them. "Father of Mercies, compose this troubled spirit: do I indeed wish it to be composed—to forget my Henry?" the my, the pen was directly drawn across in an agony.

CHAPTER XX

The mate of the ship, who heard her stir, came to offer her some refreshment; and she, who formerly received every offer of kindness or civility with pleasure, now shrunk away disgusted: peevishly she desired him not to disturb her; but the words were hardly articulated when her heart smote her, she called him back, and requested something to drink. After drinking it, fatigued by her mental exertions, she fell into a death-like slumber, which lasted some hours; but did not refresh her, on the contrary, she awoke languid and stupid.

The wind still continued contrary; a week, a dismal week, had she struggled with her sorrows; and the struggle brought on a slow fever, which sometimes gave her false spirits.

The winds then became very tempestuous, the Great Deep was troubled, and all the passengers appalled. Mary then left her bed, and went on deck, to survey the contending elements: the scene accorded with the present state of her soul; she thought in a few hours I may go home; the prisoner may be released. The vessel rose on a wave and descended into a yawning gulph—Not slower did her mounting soul return to earth, for—Ah! her treasure and her heart was there. The squalls rattled amongst the sails, which were quickly taken down; the wind would then die away, and the wild undirected waves rushed on every side with a tremendous roar. In a little vessel in the midst of such a storm she was not dismayed; she felt herself independent.

Just then one of the crew perceived a signal of distress; by the help of a glass he could plainly discover a small vessel dismasted, drifted about, for the rudder had been broken by the violence of the storm. Mary's thoughts were now all engrossed by the crew on the brink of destruction. They bore down to the wreck; they reached it, and hailed the trembling wretches; at the sound of the friendly greeting, loud cries of tumultuous joy were mixed with the roaring of the waves, and with ecstatic transport they leaped on the shattered deck, launched their boat in a moment, and committed themselves to the mercy of the sea. Stowed between two casks, and leaning on a sail, she watched the boat, and when a wave intercepted it from her view—she ceased to breathe, or rather held her breath until it rose again.

At last the boat arrived safe along-side the ship, and Mary caught the poor trembling wretches as they stumbled into it, and joined them in thanking that gracious Being, who though He had not thought fit to still the raging of the sea, had afforded them unexpected succour.

Amongst the wretched crew was one poor woman, who fainted when she was hauled on board: Mary undressed her, and when she had recovered, and soothed her, left her to enjoy the rest she required to recruit her strength, which fear had quite exhausted. She returned again to view the angry deep; and when she gazed on its perturbed state, she thought of the Being who rode on the wings of the wind, and stilled the noise of the sea; and the madness of the people—He only could speak peace to her troubled spirit! she grew more calm; the late transaction had gratified her benevolence, and stole her out of herself.

One of the sailors, happening to say to another, "that he believed the world was going to be at an end;" this observation led her into a new train of thoughts: some of Handel's sublime compositions occurred to her, and she sung them to the grand accompaniment. The Lord God Omnipotent reigned, and would reign for ever, and ever!—Why then did she fear the sorrows that were passing away, when she knew that He would bind up the broken-hearted, and receive those who came out of great tribulation. She retired to her cabin; and wrote in the little book that was now her only confident. It was after midnight.

"At this solemn hour, the great day of judgment fills my thoughts; the day of retribution, when the secrets of all hearts will be revealed; when all worldly distinctions will fade away, and be no more seen. I have not words to express the sublime images which the bare contemplation of this awful day raises in my mind. Then, indeed, the Lord Omnipotent will reign, and He will wipe the tearful eye, and support the trembling heart—yet a little while He hideth his face, and the dun shades of sorrow, and the thick clouds of folly separate us from our God; but when the glad dawn of an eternal day breaks, we shall know even as we are known. Here we walk by faith, and not by sight; and we have this alternative, either to enjoy the pleasures of life which are but for a season, or look forward to the prize of our high calling, and with fortitude, and that wisdom which is from above, endeavour to bear the warfare of life. We know that many run the race; but he that striveth obtaineth the crown of victory. Our race is an arduous one! How many are betrayed by traitors lodged in their own breasts, who wear the garb of Virtue, and are so near akin; we sigh to think they should ever lead into folly, and slide imperceptibly into vice. Surely any thing like happiness is madness! Shall probationers of an hour presume to pluck the fruit of immortality, before they have conquered death? it is guarded, when the great day, to which I allude, arrives, the way will again be opened. Ye dear delusions, gay deceits, farewell! and yet I cannot banish ye for ever; still does my panting soul push forward, and live in futurity, in the deep shades o'er which darkness hangs.—I try to pierce the gloom, and find a resting-place, where my thirst of knowledge will be gratified, and my ardent affections find an object to fix them. Every thing material must change; happiness and this fluctating principle is not compatible. Eternity, immateriality, and happiness,—what are ye? How shall I grasp the mighty and fleeting conceptions ye create?"

After writing, serenely she delivered her soul into the hands of the Father of Spirits; and slept in peace.

CHAPTER XXI

Mary rose early, refreshed by the seasonable rest, and went to visit the poor woman, whom she found quite recovered: and, on enquiry, heard that she had lately buried her husband, a common sailor; and that her only surviving child had been washed over-board the day before. Full of her own danger, she scarcely thought of her child till that was over; and then she gave way to boisterous emotions.

Mary endeavoured to calm her at first, by sympathizing with her; and she tried to point out the only solid source of comfort but in doing this she encountered many difficulties; she found her grossly ignorant, yet she did not despair: and as the poor creature could not receive comfort from the operations of her own mind, she laboured to beguile the hours, which grief made heavy, by adapting her conversation to her capacity.

There are many minds that only receive impressions through the medium of the senses: to them did Mary address herself; she made her some presents, and promised to assist her when they should arrive in England. This employment roused her out of her late stupor, and again set the faculties of her soul in motion; made the understanding contend with the imagination, and the heart throbbed not so irregularly during the contention. How short-lived was the calm! when the English coast was descried, her sorrows returned with redoubled vigor.—She was to visit and comfort the mother of her lost friend—And where then should she take up her residence? These thoughts suspended the exertions of her understanding; abstracted reflections gave way to alarming apprehensions; and tenderness undermined fortitude.

CHAPTER XXII

In England then landed the forlorn wanderer. She looked round for some few moments—her affections were not attracted to any particular part of the Island. She knew none of the inhabitants of the vast city to which she was going: the mass of buildings appeared to her a huge body without an informing soul. As she passed through the streets in an hackney-coach, disgust and horror alternately filled her mind. She met some women drunk; and the manners of those who attacked the sailors, made her shrink into herself, and exclaim, are these my fellow creatures!

Detained by a number of carts near the water-side, for she came up the river in the vessel, not having reason to hasten on shore, she saw vulgarity, dirt, and vice—her soul sickened; this was the first time such complicated misery obtruded itself on her sight.—Forgetting her own griefs, she gave the world a much indebted tear; mourned for a world in ruins. She then perceived, that great part of her comfort must arise from viewing the smiling face of nature, and be reflected from the view of innocent enjoyments: she was fond of seeing animals play, and could not bear to see her own species sink below them.

In a little dwelling in one of the villages near London, lived the mother of Ann; two of her children still remained with her; but they did not resemble Ann. To her house Mary directed the coach, and told the unfortunate mother of her loss. The poor woman, oppressed by it, and her many other cares, after an inundation of tears, began to enumerate all her past misfortunes, and present cares. The heavy tale lasted until midnight, and the impression it made on Mary's mind was so strong, that it banished sleep till towards morning; when tired nature sought forgetfulness, and the soul ceased to ruminate about many things.

She sent for the poor woman they took up at sea, provided her a lodging, and relieved her present necessities. A few days were spent in a kind of listless way; then the mother of Ann began to enquire when she thought of returning home. She had hitherto treated her with the greatest respect, and concealed her wonder at Mary's choosing a remote room in the house near the garden, and ordering some alterations to be made, as if she intended living in it.

Mary did not choose to explain herself; had Ann lived, it is probable she would never have loved Henry so fondly; but if she had, she could not have talked of her passion to any human creature. She deliberated, and at last informed the family, that she had a reason for not living with her husband, which must some time remain a secret—they stared—Not live with him! how will you live then? This was a question she could not answer; she had only about eighty pounds remaining, of the money she took with her to Lisbon; when it was exhausted where could she get more? I will work, she cried, do any thing rather than be a slave.

CHAPTER XXIII

Unhappy, she wandered about the village, and relieved the poor; it was the only employment that eased her aching heart; she became more intimate with misery—the misery that rises from poverty and the want of education. She was in the vicinity of a great city; the vicious poor in and about it must ever grieve a benevolent contemplative mind.

One evening a man who stood weeping in a little lane, near the house she resided in, caught her eye. She accosted him; in a confused manner, he informed her, that his wife was dying, and his children crying for the bread he could not earn. Mary desired to be conducted to his habitation; it was not very distant, and was the upper room in an old mansion-house, which had been once the abode of luxury. Some tattered shreds of rich hangings still remained, covered with cobwebs and filth; round the ceiling, through which the rain drop'd, was a beautiful cornice mouldering; and a spacious gallery was rendered dark by the broken windows being blocked up; through the apertures the wind forced its way in hollow sounds, and reverberated along the former scene of festivity.

It was crowded with inhabitants: som were scolding, others swearing, or singing indecent songs. What a sight for Mary! Her blood ran cold; yet she had sufficient resolution to mount to the top of the house. On the floor, in one corner of a very small room, lay an emaciated figure of a woman; a window over her head scarcely admitted any light, for the broken panes were stuffed with dirty rags. Near her were five children, all young, and covered with dirt; their sallow cheeks, and languid eyes, exhibited none of the charms of childhood. Some were fighting, and others crying for food; their yells were mixed with their mother's groans, and the wind which rushed through the passage. Mary was petrified; but soon assuming more courage, approached the bed, and, regardless of the surrounding nastiness, knelt down by the poor wretch, and breathed the most poisonous air; for the unfortunate creature was dying of a putrid fever, the consequence of dirt and want.

Their state did not require much explanation. Mary sent the husband for a poor neighbour, whom she hired to nurse the woman, and take care of the children; and then went herself to buy them some necessaries at a shop not far distant. Her knowledge of physic had enabled her to prescribe for the woman; and she left the house, with a mixture of horror and satisfaction.

She visited them every day, and procured them every comfort; contrary to her expectation, the woman began to recover; cleanliness and wholesome food had a wonderful effect; and Mary saw her rising as it were from the grave. Not aware of the danger she ran into, she did not think of it till she perceived she had caught the fever. It made such an alarming progress, that she was prevailed on to send for a physician; but the disorder was so violent, that for some days it baffled his skill; and Mary felt not her danger, as she was delirious. After the crisis, the symptoms were more favourable, and she slowly recovered, without regaining much strength or spirits; indeed they were intolerably low: she wanted a tender nurse.

For some time she had observed, that she was not treated with the same respect as formerly; her favors were forgotten when no more were expected. This ingratitude hurt her, as did a similar instance in the woman who came out of the ship. Mary had hitherto supported her; as her finances were growing low, she hinted to her, that she ought to try to earn her own subsistence: the woman in return loaded her with abuse.

Two months were elapsed; she had not seen, or heard from Henry. He was sick—nay, perhaps had forgotten her; all the world was dreary, and all the people ungrateful.

She sunk into apathy, and endeavouring to rouse herself out of it, she wrote in her book another fragment:

"Surely life is a dream, a frightful one! and after those rude, disjointed images are fled, will light ever break in? Shall I ever feel joy? Do all suffer like me; or am I framed so as to be particularly susceptible of misery? It is true, I have experienced the most rapturous emotions—short-lived delight!—ethereal beam, which only serves to shew my present misery—yet lie still, my throbbing heart, or burst; and my brain—why dost thou whirl about at such a terrifying rate? why do thoughts so rapidly rush into my mind, and yet when they disappear leave such deep traces? I could almost wish for the madman's happiness, and in a strong imagination lose a sense of woe.

"Oh! reason, thou boasted guide, why desert me, like the world, when I most need thy assistance! Canst thou not calm this internal tumult, and drive away the death-like sadness which presses so sorely on me,—a sadness surely very nearly allied to despair. I am now the prey of apathy—I could wish for the former storms! a ray of hope sometimes illumined my path; I had a pursuit; but now it visits not my haunts forlorn. Too well have I loved my fellow creatures! I have been wounded by ingratitude; from every one it has something of the serpent's tooth.

"When overwhelmed by sorrow, I have met unkindness; I looked for some one to have pity on me; but found none!—The healing balm of sympathy is denied; I weep, a solitary wretch, and the hot tears scald my cheeks. I have not the medicine of life, the dear chimera I have so often chased, a friend. Shade of my loved Ann! dost thou ever visit thy poor Mary? Refined spirit, thou wouldst weep, could angels weep, to see her struggling with passions she cannot subdue; and feelings which corrode her small portion of comfort!"

She could not write any more; she wished herself far distant from all human society; a thick gloom spread itself over her mind: but did not make her forget the very beings she wished to fly from. She sent for the poor woman she found in the garret; gave her money to clothe herself and children, and buy some furniture for a little hut, in a large garden, the master of which agreed to employ her husband, who had been bred a gardener. Mary promised to visit the family, and see their new abode when she was able to go out.

CHAPTER XXIV

Mary still continued weak and low, though it was spring, and all nature began to look gay; with more than usual brightness the sun shone, and a little robin which she had cherished during the winter sung one of his best songs. The family were particularly civil this fine morning, and tried to prevail on her to walk out. Any thing like kindness melted her; she consented.

Softer emotions banished her melancholy, and she directed her steps to the habitation she had rendered comfortable.

Emerging out of a dreary chamber, all nature looked cheerful; when she had last walked out, snow covered the ground, and bleak winds pierced her through and through: now the hedges were green, the blossoms adorned the trees, and the birds sung. She reached the dwelling, without being much exhausted and while she rested there, observed the children sporting on the grass, with improved complexions. The mother with tears thanked her deliverer, and pointed out her comforts. Mary's tears flowed not only from sympathy, but a complication of feelings and recollections the affections which bound her to her fellow creatures began again to play, and reanimated nature. She observed the change in herself, tried to account for it, and wrote with her pencil a rhapsody on sensibility.

"Sensibility is the most exquisite feeling of which the human soul is susceptible: when it pervades us, we feel happy; and could it last unmixed, we might form some conjecture of the bliss of those paradisiacal days, when the obedient passions were under the dominion of reason, and the impulses of the heart did not need correction.

"It is this quickness, this delicacy of feeling, which enables us to relish the sublime touches of the poet, and the painter; it is this, which expands the soul, gives an enthusiastic greatness, mixed with tenderness, when we view the magnificent objects of nature; or hear of a good action. The same effect we experience in the spring, when we hail the returning sun, and the consequent renovation of nature; when the flowers unfold themselves, and exhale their sweets, and the voice of music is heard in the land. Softened by tenderness; the soul is disposed to be virtuous. Is any sensual gratification to be compared to that of feelings the eves moistened after having comforted the unfortunate?

"Sensibility is indeed the foundation of all our happiness; but these raptures are unknown to the depraved sensualist, who is only moved by what strikes his gross senses; the delicate embellishments of nature escape his notice; as do the gentle and interesting affections.—But it is only to be felt; it escapes discussion."

She then returned home, and partook of the family meal, which was rendered more cheerful by the presence of a man, past the meridian of life, of polished manners, and dazzling wit. He endeavoured to draw Mary out, and succeeded; she entered into conversation, and some of her artless flights of genius struck him with surprise; he found she had a capacious mind, and that her reason was as profound as her imagination was lively. She glanced from earth to heaven, and caught the light of truth. Her expressive countenance shewed what passed in her mind, and her tongue was ever the faithful interpreter of her heart; duplicity never threw a shade over her words or actions. Mary found him a man of learning; and the exercise of her understanding would frequently make her forget her griefs, when nothing else could, except benevolence.

This man had known the mistress of the house in her youth; good nature induced him to visit her; but when he saw Mary he had another inducement. Her appearance, and above all, her genius, and cultivation of mind, roused his curiosity; but her dignified manners had such an effect on him, he was obliged to suppress it. He knew men, as well as books; his conversation was entertaining and improving. In Mary's company he doubted whether heaven was peopled with spirits masculine; and almost forgot that he had called the sex "the pretty play things that render life tolerable."

He had been the slave of beauty, the captive of sense; love he ne'er had felt; the mind never rivetted the chain, nor had the purity of it made the body appear lovely in his eyes. He was humane, despised meanness; but was vain of his abilities, and by no means a useful member of society. He talked often of the beauty of virtue; but not having any solid foundation to build the practice on, he was only a shining, or rather a sparkling character: and though his fortune enabled him to hunt down pleasure, he was discontented.

Mary observed his character, and wrote down a train of reflections, which these observations led her to make; these reflections received a tinge from her mind; the present state of it, was that kind of painful quietness which arises from reason clouded by disgust; she had not yet learned to be resigned; vague hopes agitated her.

"There are some subjects that are so enveloped in clouds, as you dissipate one, another overspreads it. Of this kind are our reasonings concerning happiness; till we are obliged to cry out with the Apostle, That it hath not entered into the heart of man to conceive in what it could consist, or how satiety could be prevented. Man seems formed for action, though the passions are seldom properly managed; they are either so languid as not to serve as a spur, or else so violent, as to overleap all bounds.

"Every individual has its own peculiar trials; and anguish, in one shape or other, visits every heart. Sensibility produces flights of virtue; and not curbed by reason, is on the brink of vice talking, and even thinking of virtue.

"Christianity can only afford just principles to govern the wayward feelings and impulses of the heart: every good disposition runs wild, if not transplanted into this soil; but how hard is it to keep the heart diligently, though convinced that the issues of life depend on it.

"It is very difficult to discipline the mind of a thinker, or reconcile him to the weakness, the inconsistency of his understanding; and a still more laborious task for him to conquer his passions, and learn to seek content, instead of happiness. Good dispositions, and virtuous propensities, without the light of the Gospel, produce eccentric characters: comet-like, they are always in extremes; while revelation resembles the laws of attraction, and produces uniformity; but too often is the attraction feeble; and the light so obscured by passion, as to force the bewildered soul to fly into void space, and wander in confusion."

CHAPTER XXV

A few mornings after, as Mary was sitting ruminating, harassed by perplexing thoughts, and fears, a letter was delivered to her: the servant waited for an answer. Her heart palpitated; it was from Henry; she held it some time in her hand, then tore it open; it was not a long one; and only contained an account of a relapse, which prevented his sailing in the first packet, as he had intended. Some tender enquiries were added, concerning her health, and state of mind; but they were expressed in rather a formal style: it vexed her, and the more so, as it stopped the current of affection, which the account of his arrival and illness had made flow to her heart—it ceased to beat for a moment—she read the passage over again; but could not tell what she was hurt by—only that it did not answer the expectations of her affection. She wrote a laconic, incoherent note in return, allowing him to call on her the next day—he had requested permission at the conclusion of his letter.

Her mind was then painfully active; she could not read or walk; she tried to fly from herself, to forget the long hours that were yet to run before to-morrow could arrive: she knew not what time he would come; certainly in the morning, she concluded; the morning then was anxiously wished for; and every wish produced a sigh, that arose from expectation on the stretch, damped by fear and vain regret.

To beguile the tedious time, Henry's favorite tunes were sung; the books they read together turned over; and the short epistle read at least a hundred times.—Any one who had seen her, would have supposed that she was trying to decypher Chinese characters.

After a sleepless night, she hailed the tardy day, watched the rising sun, and then listened for every footstep, and started if she heard the street door opened. At last he came, and she who had been counting the hours, and doubting whether the earth moved, would gladly have escaped the approaching interview.

With an unequal, irresolute pace, she went to meet him; but when she beheld his emaciated countenance, all the tenderness, which the formality of his letter had damped, returned, and a mournful presentiment stilled the internal conflict. She caught his hand, and looking wistfully at him, exclaimed, "Indeed, you are not well!"

"I am very far from well; but it matters not," added he with a smile of resignation; "my native air may work wonders, and besides, my mother is a tender nurse, and I shall sometimes see thee."

Mary felt for the first time in her life, envy; she wished involuntarily, that all the comfort he received should be from her. She enquired about the symptoms of his disorder; and heard that he had been very ill; she hastily drove away the fears, that former dear bought experience suggested: and again and again did she repeat, that she was sure he would soon recover. She would then look in his face, to see if he assented, and ask more questions to the same purport. She tried to avoid speaking of herself, and Henry left her, with a promise of visiting her the next day.

Her mind was now engrossed by one fear—yet she would not allow herself to think that she feared an event she could not name. She still saw his pale face; the sound of his voice still vibrated on her ears; she tried to retain it; she listened, looked round, wept, and prayed.

Henry had enlightened the desolate scene: was this charm of life to fade away, and, like the baseless fabric of a vision, leave not a wreck behind? These thoughts disturbed her reason, she shook her head, as if to drive them out of it; a weight, a heavy one, was on her heart; all was not well there.

Out of this reverie she was soon woke to keener anguish, by the arrival of a letter from her husband; it came to Lisbon after her departure: Henry had forwarded it to her, but did not choose to deliver it himself, for a very obvious reason; it might have produced a conversation he wished for some time to avoid; and his precaution took its rise almost equally from benevolence and love.

She could not muster up sufficient resolution to break the seal: her fears were not prophetic, for the contents gave her comfort. He informed her that he intended prolonging his tour, as he was now his own master, and wished to remain some time on the continent, and in particular to visit Italy without any restraint: but his reasons for it appeared childish; it was not to cultivate his taste, or tread on classic ground, where poets and philosophers caught their lore; but to join in the masquerades, and such burlesque amusements.

These instances of folly relieved Mary, in some degree reconciled her to herself added fuel to the devouring flame—and silenced something like a pang, which reason and conscience made her feel, when she reflected, that it is the office of Religion to reconcile us to the seemingly hard dispensations of providence; and that no inclination, however strong, should oblige us to desert the post assigned us, or force us to forget that virtue should be an active principle; and that the most desirable station, is the one that exercises our faculties, refines our affections, and enables us to be useful.

One reflection continually wounded her repose; she feared not poverty; her wants were few; but in giving up a fortune, she gave up the power of comforting the miserable, and making the sad heart sing for joy.

Heaven had endowed her with uncommon humanity, to render her one of His benevolent agents, a messenger of peace; and should she attend to her own inclinations?

These suggestions, though they could not subdue a violent passion, increased her misery. One moment she was a heroine, half determined to bear whatever fate should inflict; the next, her mind would recoil—and tenderness possessed her whole soul. Some instances of Henry's affection, his worth and genius, were remembered: and the earth was only a vale of tears, because he was not to sojourn with her.

CHAPTER XXVI

Henry came the next day, and once or twice in the course of the following week; but still Mary kept up some little formality, a certain consciousness restrained her; and Henry did not enter on the subject which he found she wished to avoid. In the course of conversation, however, she mentioned to him, that she earnestly desired to obtain a place in one of the public offices for Ann's brother, as the family were again in a declining way.

Henry attended, made a few enquiries, and dropped the subject; but the following week, she heard him enter with unusual haste; it was to inform her, that he had made interest with a person of some consequence, whom he had once obliged in a very disagreeable exigency, in a foreign country; and that he had procured a place for her friend, which would infallibly lead to something better, if he behaved with propriety. Mary could not speak to thank him; emotions of gratitude and love suffused her face; her blood eloquently spoke. She delighted to receive benefits through the medium of her fellow creatures; but to receive them from Henry was exquisite pleasure.

As the summer advanced, Henry grew worse; the closeness of the air, in the metropolis, affected his breath; and his mother insisted on his fixing on some place in the country, where she would accompany him. He could not think of going far off, but chose a little village on the banks of the Thames, near Mary's dwelling: he then introduced her to his mother.

They frequently went down the river in a boat; Henry would take his violin, and Mary would sometimes sing, or read, to them. She pleased his mother; she inchanted him. It was an advantage to Mary that friendship first possessed her heart; it opened it to all the softer sentiments of humanity:—and when this first affection was torn away, a similar one sprung up, with a still tenderer sentiment added to it.

The last evening they were on the water, the clouds grew suddenly black, and broke in violent showers, which interrupted the solemn stillness that had prevailed previous to it. The thunder roared; and the oars plying quickly, in order to reach the shore, occasioned a not unpleasing sound. Mary drew still nearer Henry; she wished to have sought with him a watry grave; to have escaped the horror of surviving him.—She spoke not, but Henry saw the workings of her mind—he felt them; threw his arm round her waist—and they enjoyed the luxury of wretchedness.—As they touched the shore, Mary perceived that Henry was wet; with eager anxiety she cried, What shall I do!—this day will kill thee, and I shall not die with thee!

This accident put a stop to their pleasurable excursions; it had injured him, and brought on the spitting of blood he was subject to—perhaps it was not the cold that he caught, that occasioned it. In vain did Mary try to shut her eyes; her fate pursued her! Henry every day grew worse and worse.

CHAPTER XXVII

Oppressed by her foreboding fears, her sore mind was hurt by new instances of ingratitude: disgusted with the family, whose misfortunes had often disturbed her repose, and lost in anticipated sorrow, she rambled she knew not where; when turning down a shady walk, she discovered her feet had taken the path they delighted to tread. She saw Henry sitting in his garden alone; he quickly opened the garden-gate, and she sat down by him.

"I did not," said he, "expect to see thee this evening, my dearest Mary; but I was thinking of thee. Heaven has endowed thee with an uncommon portion of fortitude, to support one of the most affectionate hearts in the world. This is not a time for disguise; I know I am dear to thee—and my affection for thee is twisted with every fibre of my heart.—I loved thee ever since I have been acquainted with thine: thou art the being my fancy has delighted to form; but which I imagined existed only there! In a little while the shades of death will encompass me—ill-fated love perhaps added strength to my disease, and smoothed the rugged path. Try, my love, to fulfil thy destined course—try to add to thy other virtues patience. I could have wished, for thy sake, that we could have died together— or that I could live to shield thee from the assaults of an unfeeling world! Could I but offer thee an asylum in these arms—a faithful bosom, in which thou couldst repose all thy griefs—" He pressed her to it, and she returned the pressure—he felt her throbbing heart. A mournful silence ensued! when he resumed the conversation. "I wished to prepare thee for the blow—too surely do I feel that it will not be long delayed! The passion I have nursed is so pure, that death cannot extinguish it—or tear away the impression thy virtues have made on my soul. I would fain comfort thee—"

"Talk not of comfort," interrupted Mary, "it will be in heaven with thee and Ann—while I shall remain on earth the veriest wretch!"—She grasped his hand.

"There we shall meet, my love, my Mary, in our Father's—" His voice faultered; he could not finish the sentence; he was almost suffocated—they both wept, their tears relieved them; they walked slowly to the garden-gate (Mary would not go into the house); they could not say farewel when they reached it—and Mary hurried down the lane; to spare Henry the pain of witnessing her emotions.

When she lost sight of the house she sat down on the ground, till it grew late, thinking of all that had passed. Full of these thoughts, she crept along, regardless of the descending rain; when lifting up her eyes to heaven, and then turning them wildly on the prospects around, without marking them; she only felt that the scene accorded with her present state of mind. It was the last glimmering of twilight, with a full moon, over which clouds continually flitted. Where am I wandering, God of Mercy! she thought; she alluded to the wanderings of her mind. In what a labyrinth am I lost! What miseries have I already encountered—and what a number lie still before me.

Her thoughts flew rapidly to something. I could be happy listening to him, soothing his cares.—Would he not smile upon me—call me his own Mary? I am not his—said she with fierceness—I am a wretch! and she heaved a sigh that almost broke her heart, while the big tears rolled down her burning cheeks; but still her exercised mind, accustomed to think, began to observe its operation, though the barrier of reason was almost carried away, and all the faculties not restrained by her, were running into confusion. Wherefore am I made thus? Vain are my efforts—I cannot live without loving—and love leads to madness.—Yet I will not weep; and her eyes were now fixed by despair, dry and motionless; and then quickly whirled about with a look of distraction.

She looked for hope; but found none—all was troubled waters.—No where could she find rest. I have already paced to and fro in the earth; it is not my abiding place—may I not too go home! Ah! no. Is this complying with my Henry's request, could a spirit thus disengaged expect to associate with his? Tears of tenderness strayed down her relaxed countenance, and her softened heart heaved more regularly. She felt the rain, and turned to her solitary home.

Fatigued by the tumultuous emotions she had endured, when she entered the house she ran to her own room, sunk on the bed; and exhausted nature soon closed her eyes; but active fancy was still awake, and a thousand fearful dreams interrupted her slumbers.

Feverish and languid, she opened her eyes, and saw the unwelcome sun dart his rays through a window, the curtains of which she had forgotten to draw. The dew hung on the adjacent trees, and added to the lustre; the little robin began his song, and distant birds joined. She looked; her countenance was still vacant—her sensibility was absorbed by one object.

Did I ever admire the rising sun, she slightly thought, turning from the Window, and shutting her eyes: she recalled to view the last night's scene. His faltering voice, lingering step, and the look of tender woe, were all graven on her heart; as were the words "Could these arms shield thee from sorrow—afford thee an asylum from an unfeeling world." The pressure to his bosom was not forgot. For a moment she was happy; but in a long-drawn sigh every delightful sensation evaporated. Soon—yes, very soon, will the grave again receive all I love! and the remnant of my days—she could not proceed—Were there then days to come after that?

CHAPTER XXVIII

Just as she was going to quit her room, to visit Henry, his mother called on her.

"My son is worse to-day," said she, "I come to request you to spend not only this day, but a week or two with me.—Why should I conceal any thing from you? Last night my child made his mother his confident, and, in the anguish of his heart, requested me to be thy friend—when I shall be childless. I will not attempt to describe what I felt when he talked thus to me. If I am to lose the support of my age, and be again a widow—may I call her Child whom my Henry wishes me to adopt?"

This new instance of Henry's disinterested affection, Mary felt most forcibly; and striving to restrain the complicated emotions, and sooth the wretched mother, she almost fainted: when the unhappy parent forced tears from her, by saying, "I deserve this blow; my partial fondness made me neglect him, when most he wanted a mother's care; this neglect, perhaps, first injured his constitution: righteous Heaven has made my crime its own punishment; and now I am indeed a mother, I shall loss my child—my only child!"

When they were a little more composed they hastened to the invalide; but during the short ride, the mother related several instances of Henry's goodness of heart. Mary's tears were not those of unmixed anguish; the display of his virtues gave her extreme delight—yet human nature prevailed; she trembled to think they would soon unfold themselves in a more genial clime.

CHAPTER XXIX

She found Henry very ill. The physician had some weeks before declared he never knew a person with a similar pulse recover. Henry was certain he could not live long; all the rest he could obtain, was procured by opiates. Mary now enjoyed the melancholy pleasure of nursing him, and softened by her tenderness the pains she could not remove. Every sigh did she stifle, every tear restrain, when he could see or hear them. She would boast of her resignation—yet catch eagerly at the least ray of hope. While he slept she would support his pillow, and rest her head where she could feel his breath. She loved him better than herself—she could not pray for his recovery; she could only say, The will of Heaven be done.

While she was in this state, she labored to acquire fortitude; but one tender look destroyed it all—she rather labored, indeed, to make him believe he was resigned, than really to be so.

She wished to receive the sacrament with him, as a bond of union which was to extend beyond the grave. She did so, and received comfort from it; she rose above her misery.

His end was now approaching. Mary sat on the side of the bed. His eyes appeared fixed—no longer agitated by passion, he only felt that it was a fearful thing to die. The soul retired to the citadel; but it was not now solely filled by the image of her who in silent despair watched for his last breath. Collected, a frightful calmness stilled every turbulent emotion.

The mother's grief was more audible. Henry had for some time only attended to Mary—Mary pitied the parent, whose stings of conscience increased her sorrow; she whispered him, "Thy mother weeps, disregarded by thee; oh! comfort her!—My mother, thy son blesses thee.—" The oppressed parent left the room. And Mary waited to see him die.

She pressed with trembling eagerness his parched lips—he opened his eyes again; the spreading film retired, and love returned them—he gave a look—it was never forgotten. My Mary, will you be comforted?

Yes, yes, she exclaimed in a firm voice; you go to be happy—I am not a complete wretch! The words almost choked her.

He was a long time silent; the opiate produced a kind of stupor. At last, in an agony, he cried, It is dark; I cannot see thee; raise me up. Where is Mary? did she not say she delighted to support me? let me die in her arms.

Her arms were opened to receive him; they trembled not. Again he was obliged to lie down, resting on her: as the agonies increased he leaned towards her: the soul seemed flying to her, as it escaped out of its prison. The breathing was interrupted; she heard distinctly the last sigh—and lifting up to Heaven her eyes, Father, receive his spirit, she calmly cried.

The attendants gathered round; she moved not, nor heard the clamor; the hand seemed yet to press hers; it still was warm. A ray of light from an opened window discovered the pale face.

She left the room, and retired to one very near it; and sitting down on the floor, fixed her eyes on the door of the apartment which contained the body. Every event of her life rushed across her mind with wonderful rapidity—yet all was still—fate had given the finishing stroke. She sat till midnight.—Then rose in a phrensy, went into the apartment, and desired those who watched the body to retire.

She knelt by the bed side;—an enthusiastic devotion overcame the dictates of despair.—She prayed most ardently to be supported, and dedicated herself to the service of that Being into whose hands, she had committed the spirit she almost adored—again—and again,—she prayed wildly—and fervently—but attempting to touch the lifeless hand—her head swum—she sunk—

CHAPTER XXX

Three months after, her only friend, the mother of her lost Henry began to be alarmed, at observing her altered appearance; and made her own health a pretext for travelling. These complaints roused Mary out of her torpid state; she imagined a new duty now forced her to exert herself—a duty love made sacred!—

They went to Bath, from that to Bristol; but the latter place they quickly left; the sight of the sick that resort there, they neither of them could bear. From Bristol they flew to Southampton. The road was pleasant—yet Mary shut her eyes;—or if they were open, green fields and commons, passed in quick succession, and left no more traces behind than if they had been waves of the sea.

Some time after they were settled at Southampton, they met the man who took so much notice of Mary, soon after her return to England. He renewed his acquaintance; he was really interested in her fate, as he had heard her uncommon story; besides, he knew her husband; knew him to be a good-natured, weak man. He saw him soon after his arrival in his native country, and prevented his hastening to enquire into the reasons of Mary's strange conduct. He desired him not to be too precipitate, if he ever wished to possess an invaluable treasure. He was guided by him, and allowed him to follow Mary to Southampton, and speak first to her friend.

This friend determined to trust to her native strength of mind, and informed her of the circumstance; but she overrated it: Mary was not able, for a few days after the intelligence, to fix on the mode of conduct she ought now to pursue. But at last she conquered her disgust, and wrote her husband an account of what had passed since she had dropped his correspondence.

He came in person to answer the letter. Mary fainted when he approached her unexpectedly. Her disgust returned with additional force, in spite of previous reasonings, whenever he appeared; yet she was prevailed on to promise to live with him, if he would permit her to pass one year, travelling from place to place; he was not to accompany her.

The time too quickly elapsed, and she gave him her hand—the struggle was almost more than she could endure. She tried to appear calm; time mellowed her grief, and mitigated her torments; but when her husband would take her hand, or mention any thing like love, she would instantly feel a sickness, a faintness at her heart, and wish, involuntarily, that the earth would open and swallow her.

CHAPTER XXXI

Mary visited the continent, and sought health in different climates; but her nerves were not to be restored to their former state. She then retired to her house in the country, established manufactories, threw the estate into small farms; and continually employed herself this way to dissipate care, and banish unavailing regret. She visited the sick, supported the old, and educated the young.

These occupations engrossed her mind; but there were hours when all her former woes would return and haunt her.—Whenever she did, or said, any thing she thought Henry would have approved of—she could not avoid thinking with anguish, of the rapture his approbation ever conveyed to her heart—a heart in which there was a void, that even benevolence and religion could not fill. The latter taught her to struggle for resignation; and the former rendered life supportable.

Her delicate state of health did not promise long life. In moments of solitary sadness, a gleam of joy would dart across her mind—She thought she was hastening to that world where there is neither marrying, nor giving in marriage.

Mary Wollstonecraft was born on 27th April 1759 in Spitalfields, London. Although her family had a comfortable income much was squandered by her father on speculative projects leading the family to become financially diminished and they were frequently forced to move during Wollstonecraft's youth.

The situation eventually became so dire that Wollstonecraft's father compelled her to turn over money that she would have inherited at her maturity. He was a violent man who would beat his wife in drunken rages. As a teenager, Wollstonecraft used to lie outside the door of her mother's bedroom to protect her. A valued friendship from this time was with Fanny 'Frances' Blood, who would do much to instill in Wollstonecraft the purpose of education and curiosity. The combination of these and other relationships helped to shape the volatile and depressive emotions that would haunt her life.

Unhappy with her home life, Wollstonecraft struck out on her own in 1778 and accepted a job as a lady's companion to Sarah Dawson, a widow living in Bath. In 1780 she returned home to care for her dying mother.

Rather than return to Dawson's employ after the death of her mother, Wollstonecraft moved in with the Blood family. During her two years with the family she concluded that Blood was more aligned with traditional feminine values than her own more radical viewpoint. Despite this Wollstonecraft remained dedicated to her and her family throughout her life.

Wollstonecraft had envisioned living in a female utopia with Blood; they made plans to rent rooms together and support each other emotionally and financially, but this dream soon encountered economic reality. To provide revenue Wollstonecraft, her sisters, and Blood set up a school in Newington Green, a Dissenting community. Blood was soon engaged and after marriage her husband, Hugh Skeys, took her to Lisbon, to improve her health, which had always been frail. Blood became pregnant and her health further deteriorated. In 1785 Wollstonecraft left the school and went to Lisbon to nurse her, but to no avail. Without her the school also failed.

After Blood's death, she obtained a position as governess to the daughters of the Anglo-Irish Kingsborough family in Ireland. Frustrated by the limited career options open to respectable yet poor women, she decided, after only a year as a governess, to embark upon a career as an author. This was a radical choice, since, at the time, few women could support themselves by writing.

She learned French and German and translated texts. She also wrote reviews, primarily of novels, for Johnson's periodical, the 'Analytical Review'. Wollstonecraft's intellectual universe expanded during this time, not only from the reading that she did for her reviews but also from the company she kept: she attended Johnson's famous dinners and met such luminaries as the radical pamphleteer Thomas Paine and the philosopher William Godwin. Despite their future marriage they were initially disappointed in each other.

While in London, Wollstonecraft pursued a relationship with the married artist Henry Fuseli. She was, she wrote, enraptured by his genius, 'the grandeur of his soul, that quickness of comprehension, and lovely sympathy'. Boldly she proposed a platonic living arrangement with Fuseli and his wife. Fuseli's wife was shocked and the relationship was immediately severed.

Wollstonecraft decided to travel to France to escape further humiliation and to take part in the revolutionary events that she had just celebrated in her recent 'Vindication of the Rights of Men' (1790) that had brought her immediate fame. She called the French Revolution a 'glorious chance to obtain more virtue and happiness than hitherto blessed our globe'.

Wollstonecraft was now being compared with such leading lights as the theologian and controversialist Joseph Priestley and Thomas Paine. She left for Paris in December 1792 and arrived about a month before Louis XVI was guillotined. Britain and France were now on the brink of war. France was in turmoil. She sought out other British visitors and joined the circle of expatriates then in Paris. During her time in Paris, she chose to keep company mostly with the moderate Girondins rather than the more radical Jacobins.

On 26th December 1792, Wollstonecraft saw the former king, Louis XVI, being taken to be tried before the National Assembly, and much to her own surprise, found 'the tears flow insensibly from my eyes, when I saw Louis sitting, with more dignity than I expected from his character, in a hackney coach going to meet death, where so many of his race have triumphed'.

France declared war on Britain in February 1793 and Wollstonecraft tried to leave for Switzerland but was denied permission.

Life became very difficult for foreigners in France. Despite her sympathy for the revolution, life for Wollstonecraft was increasingly stressed.

Having just written the 'Rights of Woman', Wollstonecraft determined to put her ideas to the test in the intellectual cauldron of the French Revolution. She alighted on and fell passionately in love with Gilbert Imlay, an American diplomat and adventurer. Wollstonecraft put her own principles into practice by sleeping with Imlay, which was deemed unacceptable behavior from a 'respectable' British woman. She appears to have fallen in love with an idealisation of the man who had no interest in marrying her. Wollstonecraft was now conflicted. She had rejected the sexual element in the 'Rights of Woman', but now found that Imlay had awakened her interest in sex.

Wollstonecraft was certainly disillusioned to find that that reality for women and aspiration were two separate things. She wrote that the people under the republic still behaved slavishly to those who held power while the government remained 'venal' and 'brutal'. She was offended by the Jacobins' treatment of women. They refused to grant women equal rights, denounced 'Amazons', and made it clear that women were supposed to conform to Jean-Jacques Rousseau's ideal of helpers to men.

As the daily arrests and executions of the Reign of Terror began, Wollstonecraft too came under suspicion. She was, after all, a British citizen known to be a friend of leading Girondins. On 31st October 1793, most of the Girondin leaders were guillotined; when Imlay broke the news to Wollstonecraft, she fainted.

By this time, Imlay was sensing commercial advantage in the British blockade of France, which had caused shortages and worsened ever-growing inflation. He chartered ships to bring food and essentials from America and dodge the British Royal Navy. On arrival these goods could be sold at inflated prices to those who still had money. Imlay's blockade-running gained the respect of the Jacobins, ensuring, as he had hoped, his freedom during the Terror.

To protect Wollstonecraft from the prospect of arrest, Imlay made a false statement to the U.S. embassy in Paris that he had married her, automatically making her an American citizen.

Wollstonecraft, now pregnant by Imlay, gave birth to her first child, Fanny, on 14th May 1794. She was overjoyed.

Imlay, unhappy with the domestic-minded and maternal Wollstonecraft, now left. He promised that he would return to her and Fanny at Le Havre, but his delays in writing to her and his long absences convinced Wollstonecraft otherwise.

In July 1794, Wollstonecraft welcomed the fall of the Jacobins, hoping it would be followed by a restoration of freedom of the press in France. She returned to Paris but the following month Imlay departed for London. Wollstonecraft, fearing for her liberty in Britain, dared not go with him. The British government had begun a crackdown on radicals, suspending civil liberties, imposing drastic censorship, and trying for treason anyone suspected of sympathy with the revolution.

The winter of 1794–95 was the coldest winter in over a century. Wollstonecraft and Fanny were reduced to desperate circumstances. The river Seine froze, which made it impossible for ships to bring food and coal to Paris, leading to widespread starvation and deaths from the cold in the city.

'An Historical and Moral View of the French Revolution' was first published in London in 1794. Wollstonecraft was not trained as a historian, but she used journals, letters and documents to recount how the ordinary people in France reacted to the revolution. She was trying to counteract the general British view that the entire French nation was going mad. Wollstonecraft argued instead that the revolution errupted due to a set of social, economic and political conditions that left no other solution to the crisis that gripped France in 1789.

Nonetheless 'An Historical and Moral View of the French Revolution' was a difficult balancing act for Wollstonecraft. She condemned the Jacobin regime and the Reign of Terror, but argued in parallel that the revolution was a great achievement. Conveniently she chose to end her history in late 1789 rather than write about the Terror of 1793–94.

Wollstonecraft now had to risk leaving France and did so on 7th April 1795. She also referred to herself as 'Mrs Imlay', even to her sisters, in order to bestow legitimacy upon her Fanny. She sought Imlay out but he was impassive to her pleas. In May 1795 she attempted to commit suicide, probably with laudanum, but it is thought Imlay saved her life. In a last throw of the dice to win him back, she embarked upon some business negotiations for him in Scandinavia, in order to recoup some of the losses his projects had encountered. She took this hazardous trip with only Fanny and a maid. She recounted her travels and thoughts in letters to Imlay, which were later collated and published as 'Letters Written During a Short Residence in Sweden, Norway, and Denmark' in 1796.

When she returned to England it was now certain that her relationship with Imlay was over. She attempted suicide for the second time. She proceeded to go out on a rainy night and gaining the weight of sodden clothes jumped into the River Thames. But a passing stranger witnessed her jump and rescued her.

For Wollstonecraft the suicide attempt was deeply rational, writing after her rescue:—

"I have only to lament, that, when the bitterness of death was past, I was inhumanly brought back to life and misery. But a fixed determination is not to be baffled by disappointment; nor will I allow that to be a frantic attempt, which was one of the calmest acts of reason. In this respect, I am only accountable to myself. Did I care for what is termed reputation, it is by other circumstances that I should be dishonoured."

Gradually, Wollstonecraft returned to literary life, becoming involved with Joseph Johnson's circle again, in particular with Mary Hays, Elizabeth Inchbald, and Sarah Siddons through William Godwin.

Godwin and Wollstonecraft's courtship began slowly, but eventually became a passionate love affair. Godwin had read her 'Letters Written in Sweden, Norway, and Denmark' and later wrote that "If ever there was a book calculated to make a man in love with its author, this appears to me to be the book. She speaks of her sorrows, in a way that fills us with melancholy, and dissolves us in tenderness, at the same time that she displays a genius which commands all our admiration."

Once Wollstonecraft became pregnant by him, they decided to marry so that the child would be legitimate. Unfortunately, that marriage now revealed that Wollstonecraft had never been married to Imlay, and, as a result, they lost many in their circle. After their marriage on 29th March 1797, Godwin and Wollstonecraft moved to Somers Town, in London. Godwin also rented a nearby apartment in Chalton Street as a study, giving both a measure of independence. By all accounts, it was a happy and stable marriage.

On 30th August 1797, Wollstonecraft gave birth to her second daughter, Mary. During the delivery seemed the placenta broke apart and became infected. Childbed fever was a common but often fatal occurrence in the eighteenth century.

After several days of agony, Mary Wollstonecraft died of septicemia on 10th September 1797. She was 38.

She was buried at Old Saint Pancras Churchyard, where her tombstone reads,

"Mary Wollstonecraft Godwin, Author of A Vindication of the Rights of Woman: Born 27 April 1759: Died 10 September 1797."

In 1851, her remains were moved by her grandson Percy Florence Shelley to his family tomb in St Peter's Church, Bournemouth.

Mary Wollstonecraft – A Concise Bibliography

Thoughts on the Education of Daughters: With Reflections on Female Conduct, in the More Important Duties of Life (1787)
Mary: A Fiction (1788)
Original Stories from Real Life: With Conversations Calculated to Regulate the Affections and Form the Mind to Truth and Goodness (1788)
A Vindication of the Rights of Men, in a Letter to the Right Honourable Edmund Burke. (1790)
A Vindication of the Rights of Woman with Strictures on Moral and Political Subjects (1792)

An Historical and Moral View of the French Revolution; and the Effect It Has produced in Europe (1794)
Letters Written during a Short Residence in Sweden, Norway, and Denmark (1796)
On Poetry, and Our Relish for the Beauties of Nature (Monthly Magazine April 1797)
The Wrongs of Woman, or Maria. Posthumous Works of the Author of A Vindication of the Rights of Woman. Ed. William Godwin (1798. Published posthumously; unfinished)
The Cave of Fancy". Posthumous Works of the Author of A Vindication of the Rights of Woman. Ed. William Godwin (1798. Published posthumously; fragment written in 1787)
Letter on the Present Character of the French Nation. Posthumous Works of the Author of A Vindication of the Rights of Woman. Ed. William Godwin (1798. Published posthumously; written in 1793)
Fragment of Letters on the Management of Infants". Posthumous Works of the Author of A Vindication of the Rights of Woman. Ed. William Godwin (1798. Published posthumously; unfinished)
Lessons". Posthumous Works of the Author of A Vindication of the Rights of Woman. Ed. William Godwin (1798. Published posthumously; unfinished)
Hints". Posthumous Works of the Author of A Vindication of the Rights of Woman. Ed. William Godwin. (1798. Published posthumously; notes on the second volume of Rights of Woman, never written)
Contributions to the Analytical Review (1788–1797. Published anonymously)

Translations

Of the Importance of Religious Opinions. Jacques Necker (1788)
The Female Reader: Or, Miscellaneous Pieces, in Prose and Verse; selected from the best writers, and disposed under proper heads; for the improvement of young women. Mr. Cresswick, teacher of elocution (1789)
Young Grandison. A Series of Letters from Young Persons to Their Friends. Maria Geertruida van de Werken de Cambon. (1790)
Elements of Morality, for the Use of Children; with an introductory address to parents Christian Gotthilf Salzmann. (1790)